THE SNOW-WALKER'S SON

Gudrun turned away. 'Take them out.'

'Wait!'

Every eye turned to Thorkil; men who had been talking fell silent. 'Don't you mind?' he asked, his fingers clenched on the ring. 'That we'll see? That we're going there . . .?' Despite himself he could not finish.

Jessa saw a movement in the corner; it was the old man, Grettir. He had turned his head and was watching.

Gudrun stared straight at Thorkil. All she said was, 'Thrasirshall is the pit where I fling my rubbish.' She stepped close to him; he shivered in the coldness that came out from her.

'I want you to see him. I'll enjoy thinking of it. I'll enjoy watching your face, because I will see it, however far away you think me. Even in the snows and the wilderness nothing hides from me.'

She glanced down, and his eyes followed hers. He had gripped the ring so tight the serpent's mouth had cut him. One drop of blood ran down his fingers.

By the same author

The Conjuror's Game
Fintan's Tower

Catherine Fisher

—

THE SNOW-WALKER'S SON

RED FOX

The quotations, which head the chapters and are reprinted here with the kind permission from the publisher, are from 'The Words of the High One', a poem that appears in *Norse Poems*, edited and translated by W. H. Auden and Paul B. Taylor; Faber and Faber Ltd, 1983.

A Red Fox Book

Published by Random House Children's Books
20 Vauxhall Bridge Road, London SW1V 2SA

A division of Random House UK Ltd

London Melbourne Sydney Auckland
Johannesburg and agencies throughout the world

First published in 1993 by The Bodley Head Ltd

Red Fox edition 1994

3 5 7 9 10 8 6 4 2

Printed and bound in Great Britain by
Cox & Wyman Ltd, Reading, Berkshire

RANDOM HOUSE UK Limited Reg. No. 954009

ISBN 0 09 919351 5

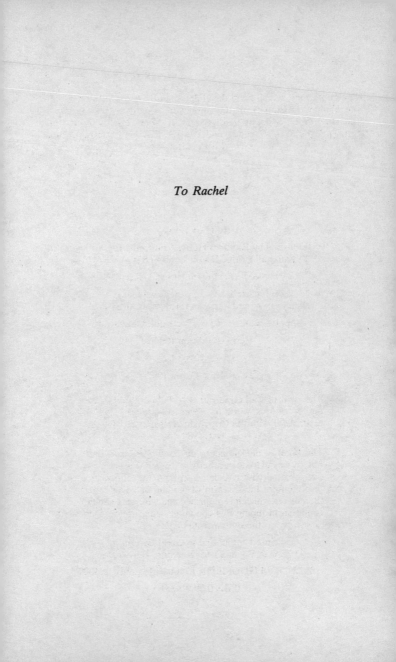

To Rachel

The door was the last one in the corridor.

As the flames flickered over it they showed it was barred; a hefty iron chain hung across it, and the mud floor beneath was red with rust that had flaked off in the long years of locking and unlocking.

The keeper hung his lantern on a nail, took the key from a dirty string around his neck, and fitted it into the keyhole. Then he looked behind him.

'Get on with it!' the big man growled. 'Let me see what she keeps in there!'

The keeper grinned; he knew fear when he heard it. With both hands he turned the key, then tugged out the red chain in a shower of rust and pushed the door. It opened, just a fraction. Darkness and a damp smell oozed through the black slit.

He stepped well back, handed the stranger the lantern, and jerked his head. He had no tongue to speak with; she'd made sure he kept her secrets.

The stranger hesitated; a draught moved his hair and he gazed back up the stone passageway as if he longed suddenly for warmth and light. And from what I've heard, the keeper thought, you won't be seeing much of those ever again.

Then the man held up the lantern and pushed the

door. The keeper watched his face intently in the red glow, and his great hand, as it clutched a luck-stone that swung at his neck. The man went in, slowly. The door closed.

Outside, the keeper waited, listening. No sound came out of the room and he dared not go too close. For six years now he had locked it and unlocked it, letting in the witch Gudrun and the sly old dwarf she brought with her. No one else in all that time – until today, this gruff red-beard.

For six years he had left food at the door and taken it away half eaten; had heard rustles and move-ments and had never looked in. But there had been that night, nearly a year ago now, when halfway up the corridor he had looked back, and in the dimness seen that hand, thin as a claw, lifting the platter.

Suddenly the door opened; he stiffened, his hand on his knife. The big man was there, carrying some-thing heavy, wrapped in old bearskins. He cradled it with both arms; whatever it was moved in the heavy folds against his shoulder. It made a low sound, wordless and strange.

The man had changed. His face was pale, his voice quiet. 'Tell her,' he muttered through his teeth, 'that her secret is safe with me. I'll keep it better than she did.'

Shoving the keeper aside, he strode through the flames and shadows of the stone tunnel.

The keeper waited; waited until the echoes of dis-tant chains and gates were still. Then, furtively, he slid his lantern around the door and looked into the room.

He saw a small cell, with one window high up in the wall, icicles hanging from its sill; a low bed;

straw; a fireplace full of ashes. He stepped in, warily. There were a few scraps of food on the floor, but nothing to give any sign of what had been here.

It was only when he turned to go that his eyes caught the patterns: the rows and rows of strange, whirling spirals scrawled on the damp wall next to the bed.

Young and alone on a long road,
Once I lost my way:
Rich I felt when I found another . . .

The Hall was empty.

Jessa edged inside and began to wander idly about, pulling the thick furred collar of her coat up around her face. She was early.

It had been a bitter night. The snow had blown in under the door and spread across the floor. A pool of wine that someone had spilt under the table was frozen to a red slab. She nudged it with her foot; solid as glass. Even the spiders were dead on their webs; the thin nets shook in the draught.

She walked to the great pillar of oak that grew up through the middle of the Hall. It was heavily carved with old runes and magic signs, but over them all, obliterating them, was a newer cutting: a contorted snake that twisted itself down in white spirals. She brushed the frost off it with her gloved fingers. The snake was Gudrun's sign. A witch's sign.

She waited, grinding the ice to white powder under her heel.

Light gathered, slowly. Corners of tables and tapestries loomed out of the shadows; a cart rumbled by outside, and the carter's shout echoed in the roof.

Jessa kicked the frozen fire. Why hadn't she come late – sauntered in sweetly when the Jarl was waiting, just to show him that she didn't care, that he couldn't order her as he wanted? It was too late now, though.

Five slow minutes slithered by.

Then, a hanging was flipped back; a house-thrall came in and began to take down the shutters. Frost cracked and fell from the empty windows; a raw wind whipped in and rippled the tapestries.

He hadn't seen her. Jessa was annoyed. She shuffled, and watched him whirl around, his face white. Then the terror drained out of him. That annoyed her even more.

'I'm waiting to speak to the Lord Jarl,' she snapped, in a clear voice. 'My name is Jessa Horolfsdaughter.'

It was the voice she always used with servants, cold and rather distant. Old Marrika, her nurse, used to say it was the voice of pride. What was Marrika doing now? she wondered.

The man nodded and went out. Jessa scuffed the floor impatiently. She hated this place. Everyone in it was afraid. They were littered with amulets and luckstones; they glanced around before they spoke, as if someone was always listening. Gudrun. The Jarl's strange wife. The Snow-walker. They said she knew what you thought, even as you stood before her. Jessa shivered.

The man came back and knelt at the hearth. She saw the welcome flicker of flames and hurried over, warming her hands and rubbing them against her face until her cheeks ached. The thrall propped some logs on the blaze and went out. Jessa did not speak to him. People said all the Jarl's servants were dumb. Whatever the truth of that, they never spoke.

Crouched over the fire, she looked down the high Hall. The trestles and stools were toppled here and there on the straw. At the far end was a raised platform; here the seats were piled with red cushions, the table littered with half-empty plates. Jessa went over and picked up a pewter jug. The wine in it was frozen. She put it down with a bang.

As she turned, one of the tapestries behind the dais was drawn aside and an elderly man came in, with a boy of her own age behind him. She knew the boy at once. Thorkil Harraldsson was her first cousin; they'd brought him here about three months ago. His clothes were very fine, she thought, scornfully. Just like him.

The other was Jarl Ragnar. He was still tall, but his shoulders stooped; the splendid blue quilted robe hung loose on him. He looked like a man dried out, sucked dry of all life, his eyes small and cold.

She made him the most careless bow she could.

'You have your father's manners,' he said, wryly.

Silent, she watched Thorkil drag up two stools and the Jarl's chair; he caught her eye and gave her a brief, wan smile. She thought he seemed uneasy, and very pleased to see her. No wonder. Prison was prison, even with fine clothes.

They sat down. The Jarl stared into the flames. Finally he spoke, without looking at them.

'Your fathers were two brothers. I had thought they were loyal to me, until they joined that last foolish march of the Wulfings. All my enemies together. It was a pity they both died in the snow.'

Jessa glared at him. 'Your wife's sorcery brought the snow. She won your battle for you.'

He was angry, but Jessa didn't care. 'The Lord Jarl has always come from the family of the Wulfings. That's why they fought you. You have no right to be Jarl.'

She caught Thorkil's nervous, warning look, but it was done now. She had said it. Her face was hot, her hands shook.

Grimly, the Jarl stared at the flames. 'The family of the Wulfings are almost all gone,' he said. 'Those that are left lurk in farms and steads and byres, their women and children disguised as thralls, hurried indoors when riders come by. Gudrun knows. She sees them. One by one, I am hunting them out. The leader, Wulfgar, was taken two days ago; he's in a room under your feet, with ice and rats for company. And now there's you.'

His hands rubbed together, dry as paper.

'I left you alone. I left you on your farms, fed you and let you be, until now. Now, you are old enough to be dangerous.'

Jessa watched his eyes on the leaping flames. She wanted him to turn and look at her, but he would not.

'Your land will be given to men loyal to me, and you will have somewhere else to live.'

'Here?' Thorkil asked.

'Not here.' He smiled briefly. 'Far from here.'

Jessa was glad. She had been here two days and that was enough. But she didn't trust that smile.

'Where then?'

The Jarl moved, as if he was suddenly uneasy.

8

The silver amulets and thorshammers round his neck clicked together.

'I'm sending you to live with my son,' he said.

For a moment they couldn't realize what he meant. Then Jessa felt sick; cold sweat prickled on her back. Slowly her hand sought the amulet Marrika had given her.

Thorkil was white. 'You can't send us there,' he breathed.

'Hold your tongue and let me finish.' Ragnar was looking at them now, with a hard, amused stare.

'Your fathers were traitors; they wanted to bring me down. Many men remember them. Do you expect me to set you up on farms, to give you herds of reindeer and dowries of silver?'

'Why not?' Jessa muttered. 'You took ours.'

He laughed. 'Call it exile, and think yourselves lucky. At least you'll have a sort of life. You leave tomorrow for Thrasirshall, at first light. I'll supply a ship and an escort, at least as far as Trond. I don't suppose my men will want to go further.'

Jessa saw Thorkil was trembling. She knew he couldn't believe this; he was terrified. It burst out of him in a wild, despairing cry.

'I won't go! You can't send us out there, not to that creature!'

With one swift movement the Jarl stood and struck him in the face with the full weight of his glove, so that he staggered back on the stool and fell with a crash on the stone floor. Jessa grabbed him, but he shrugged her off. Tears of fury glinted in his eyes as he scrambled up.

'Take a lesson from your cousin,' the Jarl said.

9

'Look your fate in the eye. I'd thought you were stronger, but I see you're still a boy.'

Jessa took Thorkil's wrist and held it tight. Better to keep quiet now.

The Jarl watched them. 'Gudrun is right,' he said. 'Traitors breed traitors.'

Then, slowly, he sat down, and ran one hand wearily down one cheek.

'There's something else.'

'What?' Jessa asked coldly.

He took something from inside his coat and held it out: a thick piece of sealskin. She saw the blue veins in his skin.

'It's a message.' Ragnar looked at them, almost reluctantly, 'I want you to take it with you. It's for Brochael Gunnarsson . . . the man who looks after the creature. Give it to him. Tell no one.' He looked wearily around the empty hall. 'Whatever sort of thing Kari is, he is my son.

There was silence. Then he said, 'Take it.'

For a long moment Jessa did not move. Then she reached out and took the parcel. The parchment inside it crackled as she slid it into her glove.

The Jarl nodded, and stood up, straightening slowly. He walked a few steps and then stopped. Without looking back he said, 'Come here tonight, after the lawgiving. Gudrun wishes to speak to you. There's nothing I can do about it.'

He looked over his shoulder at them. 'Keep my secret. I can do nothing else for Kari. Maybe, years ago, if I had tried . . . but not now. She would know.' He smiled at them, a bitter smile. 'I've never seen him. I do not know what he is.'

In the silence after he had shuffled out, a pigeon

fluttered in the roof. One glossy feather whirled down through a shaft of light.

'Why did you take it?' Thorkil asked.

Jessa was wondering too. 'Not so loud,' she murmured.

He went to the fire and knelt near the dirty hearth; Jessa followed. 'We must escape.'

'Where?'

'Your farm – Horolfstead.'

'His men have got it.' She pulled at her glove. 'Three days ago.'

Thorkil glanced at her. 'I should have known. Well, why bother to talk? There's nothing we can do – he's sending men with us.'

'To Thrasirshall.'

'Mmm.'

Jessa was silent for a moment. Then she glanced round. 'Thorkil . . .'

'What?' But he knew what.

'You've been here longer than I have. What do they say here about Kari Ragnarsson?'

'Nothing. No one dares.' Thorkil dropped his voice. 'Besides, no one has ever seen him, except the woman who was there when he was born. She died a few days later. They say Gudrun poisoned her.'

Jessa nodded. 'Yes, but there are rumours . . .'

'The same as you've heard.' Thorkil edged nearer to the fire. 'She kept him locked up here somewhere, in a windowless room. He has a pelt of fur like a troll. He tears his skin with his teeth in his fits. Others say he has eyes like a wolf. There are plenty of stories. Who knows which is true? Now she keeps him in the ruin called Thrasirshall. They say it's at

11

the edge of the world, far out in the snowfields. No one has ever been there.'

She stood up. 'Neither will we. We'll get away. How can they watch us all the time?'

'Gudrun can. And where can we go in a wilderness of ice?'

But Jessa had crouched suddenly, her gloved fingers on his lips. 'Quiet!'

Together, they turned their heads. The hanging on the far wall was rippling slightly; the faded bears and hunters stitched on it seemed to move under the dirt.

'Someone's there,' Jessa whispered. 'Someone's been listening to us.'

2

Shun a woman wise in magic.

They waited, for a long minute. Then Thorkil walked over and carefully pushed the musty cloth. It gave under his hand.

'There's a space here,' he muttered. 'No wall.'

As there was no sound he pulled the deep folds of the hanging apart and slipped inside; after a quick look round Jessa followed. In the dimness they saw a stone archway in the wall, and beyond that a staircase twisting up. Footsteps were climbing it, lightly.

'I told you,' Jessa whispered. 'Who is it?'

'I don't know. Probably. . . .' Then he stopped.

Behind them, someone had come into the Hall, someone silent, without footsteps, someone who froze the air. Jessa felt sudden crystals harden on her face and mouth; felt a cold numbness that pierced her skin. Thorkil was still; frost glistened on his lips.

'It's Gudrun,' he breathed.

And as if the walker on the stairs had heard him, the footsteps stopped, and began to come back down.

Suddenly, Jessa had never felt so afraid. Her heart thudded; she wanted to run, had to fight to hold herself still, clenching her fingers into fists. Before them the footsteps came closer; behind in the Hall some terrible coldness loomed. Grabbing at Thorkil she tugged him between the heavy tapestries and the wall; there was a black slit there, filthy with dust. Something brushed his coat; the tapestry whirled, and a small bent figure, much muffled in cloaks and coats, slipped past them into the Hall.

'Gudrun,' they heard him say, 'you move like a ghost.'

'But you heard me.'

'I felt you.'

Their voices withdrew into the room. Coldness ebbed, the freezing fear slowly loosened its grip. Jessa heard Thorkil's shudder of breath; saw his hand was shaking as he gently moved aside a fold of the cloth, so they could see part of the Hall.

Someone was sitting in the Jarl's chair, looking no more than a bundle of rich fabrics. Then he pushed his hood back, and Jessa saw it was a very old man, thin and spry, his hair wisps of white, his look sly and sidelong.

'They leave tomorrow,' he was saying. 'As you expected.'

Astonished, Jessa stared at Thorkil.

The woman laughed, a low peal of sound that made a new surge of fear leap in Jessa's stomach.

The old man chuckled too. 'And they know all about Thrasirshall, the poor waifs.'

'What do they know?' she said.

'Oh, that the wind howls through it, that it's a wilderness of trolls and spirits on the edge of the world. Not to speak of what the Hall contains.' He spat, and then grinned.

They could just see the woman's white hands, and

her sleeves. Gently, Thorkil edged the curtain a little wider.

Gudrun stood in the light from the window. She was tall and young, her skin white as a candle; her hair pure blonde and braided in long intricate braids down her back. Her ice-blue dress was edged with fur. Silver glittered at wrist and throat; she stood straight, her sharp gaze towards them. Jessa felt Thorkil's instant stillness. Even from here, they could see her eyes had no colour.

'How did they take their news?'

'The girl, quietly. Master Thorkil squealed, but Ragnar stopped that.'

Gudrun laughed. 'Even the Jarl needs his pleasures. I allow him a few.'

'But there is one thing you may not know.'

Her eyes turned on him. 'Be careful,' she said lightly. 'Even you, Grettir.'

He seemed to shift uneasily in the chair. Then he said, 'Ragnar gave the girl a letter. It was for Brochael Gunnarsson. It was a warning.'

She laughed again, a murmur of amusement. 'Is that all? What good will that do? Let them take it, by all means.' With a rustle of silks she moved to sit by him; Thorkil edged the curtain to keep her in sight.

'None of it matters.' She rested her white fingers lightly on the old man's shoulder. 'Everything is ready. Ragnar is sending them there because I slid the idea of it into his mind, just as he speaks my words and eats and sleeps as I allow him.'

'But the letter?'

She shrugged. 'He has a corner of himself left

15

alive. As for those two, I have my own plans for them.'

She put her lips near his ear; dropped her voice low. Jessa strained to hear. 'I'll have my hand on them,' the woman said. Then she whispered something that made the old man grin and shake his head slyly. 'You have the great powers, Gudrun. Not many can touch you.'

Instantly, he was silent, as if he knew he had made a mistake. She leaned forward and ran the sharp point of one fingernail gently down his cheek. To her horror Jessa saw it leave a trail of white ice that cracked and fell away; a blue scar in the skin as if some intense cold had seared it. The old man moaned, and clutched his face.

Gudrun smiled. 'Be careful, Grettir. No one can touch me. No one.'

She ran her fingers lightly through his hair. 'Remember that.'

She got up and wandered to the table, then to the fire. 'As for the creature in Thrasirshall, you and I know what he is.'

She stretched one hand over the flames; thrust it close. Jessa saw a single drop of clear liquid fall from the white fingers, as if, she thought, they had begun to melt in the heat. As the drop hit the flames they hissed and crackled, leaping into a tower of fire. Smoke drifted round the Hall; it hung in long snakes that moved around the woman's waist and feet, slithering over the flagged floor, blurring sight, so that to Jessa the fire faded to a halo of red, and Gudrun and Grettir were shadows without edges. Staring hard, she thought she saw something form among the flames, the dim outline of a building, a window, a room full of light, and someone sitting there, turning his head . . .

Then the door of the Hall slammed open. The thrall that Jessa had met earlier stood in the doorway, his arms full of wood. He stopped, frozen in terror.

Gudrun whirled in the smoke. She was furious; snakes of grey mist coiled and surged around her. 'Out!' she hissed, her voice hoarse with rage.

The man stood there, rooted, as if he dared not move. Jessa felt a pang of fear shoot through her – Get out! she thought, but he stayed, staring with horror at Gudrun as she jerked her hand towards him.

Logs cascaded to the floor with hollow smacks of sound. The man crumpled, soundless. He crouched on his knees, sobbing and shaking. Gudrun walked up to him. She stood a moment, looking down, then bent and lifted his chin. Pain convulsed him; he shuddered as she ran her long fingers across his throat. 'Out,' she whispered.

He staggered up, and crashed through the door. They could hear the echoes of his flight a long time, hanging in the smoky air.

Jessa breathed out with relief, but at the same time she touched the edge of the tapestry, and it rippled and swished. Instantly, Thorkil dropped it and flattened himself against the wall. There was silence in the Hall. Jessa's heart thumped against her ribs.

Then Gudrun spoke. She was so close that Jessa almost jumped.

'Kari won't escape me, either. I've let him be far too long, to see what he would become. And yet,

17

Grettir' – her voice turned away from them – 'I have almost a desire to see him, to taste him, to use what he has.'

Her hand came round the tapestry. Jessa almost screamed. The white fingers were inches from her face.

'But they'll be here tonight, both of those two. That will be my time.'

Grettir must have moved; they heard his chair scrape the flagstones.

'I will come.'

'You must please yourself, old man, as ever.' Then she turned and flashed past them, under the archway and up the stairs, her light steps rising into silence above them.

Thorkil let his breath out in a gasp and clutched Jessa's arm. They were stifled; both wanted to run out, to breathe clean air, but the old man was still there, standing silently by his chair. Slowly, he crossed to the courtyard door and unlatched it. Cold air rippled the tapestries to a storm of dust. When Jessa had wiped her eyes and peered out, the Hall was empty.

They ran straight to the door, squeezed through, and closed it. Smoke coiled out after them, dissipating in the wind. The watchman, half asleep, stared at their backs as they walked, too quickly, between the houses, among the children and the squalling hens. Once Jessa turned, feeling herself watched, but the windows of the Jarlshold were dark and empty.

3

With a good man it is good to talk,
Make him your fast friend.

' "I'll have my hand on them." And she meant us.'
Jessa watched Mord Signi stack the slabs of peat
carefully on to the back of the fire, and jerk his hand
out as the sparks leapt. 'What do you think she
meant?'

'I don't think,' Mord said, straightening. 'Not
about her.'

He was a tall man; his grey hair brushed the low
turf roof. He glanced over at his wife, folding Jessa's
clothes into a leather bag. 'But I can't let this go.
Not without a murmur.'

She put her hand on his shoulder. 'It's no use
talking to Ragnar,' she said quietly. 'Why should he
listen?' Then she bent forward and whispered, so
that Jessa only just caught the words. 'Stay out of it.
You have your own children to think of.'

He turned aside, silent. Jessa felt sorry for him.
He had been a kinsman of her father; he was a
marked man in the Jarlshold. And his wife was right.
No pleading would move Ragnar, and anyway, she,
Jessa, wouldn't have it.

Mord came back to the fire. The hearth was a
large, square one in the middle of the house, and

around the walls were the sleeping booths, with their wooden screens and warm, musty hangings. By now the fire was a hot blaze, licking and spitting over the new peats, throwing glows and shadows around the room, over Thorkil's face, and Mord's, worried and upset. Outside, the afternoon sky was darkening with snow. Winter lingered late, as usual, in the Jarlshold.

Thorkil said, 'Mord, tell us about Gudrun.'

'Best not to, lad. I'd rather keep my tongue.'

'But we need to know.' Thorkil glanced at Mord's wife, with her youngest daughter pulling at her skirts. 'We're going there, after all.'

She turned away from him. 'He's right, Mord.'

Mord put down the peat he had been crumbling, got up slowly and locked the door. Coming back, he sat closer to the fire.

'It's a stranger story than any skald's saga. Much of it you'll know, I'm sure. When Ragnar was a young man the Wulfings were the ruling kin in the North. He was just one of many small landowners; your fathers were two more. But he was ambitious. He bought land where he could, stole it where he couldn't, ruined his enemies in the Althing (that was the old law court) and gathered ruthless, cruel men about him. Still, he might have stayed as he was, if it hadn't been for her.'

Mord paused. Then he said, 'Beyond the Yngvir River and the mountains there's only ice. It stretches, they say, to the edge of the world, into the endless blackness. Travellers – those that have come back – speak of great cracks that open underfoot, of mountains smooth as glass, of the sky catching fire. Beyond the icebergs even the sea freezes.

No animals live there, not even the white bears, though I have heard a tale of a long glistening worm that burrows in the ice. It may not be true. But certainly there are trolls, and ettins, and some sort of spirit that howls in the empty crevasses.

'In those lands live the White People, the Snow-walkers, a race of wizards. No one knows much about them, except that sometimes they would come to the northern borders and raid. Children would disappear from farms, and it would be said that the White People had taken them. Cattle too, and some-times dogs.

'One year the raids were so bad the old Jarl sent Ragnar with a warband to march up there and settle it. They crossed the hills by way of the old giant's road that passes Thrasirshall, and marched down the other side, straight into a white mist. It was waiting for them there, a solid whiteness that even the wind couldn't blow away. Fifty men marched into that devil's trap, and only one came out.'

'What was it?' Thorkil asked.

'Sorcery. Rune-magic.' Mord shrugged. 'Who knows? But three months later a ship came into the harbour at Tarva, a strange ship with dark sails and twenty oarsmen – tall white-haired men who spoke a fluid, unknown language. The old man, Grettir, led them – he was younger then, of course. Then Ragnar came out of the ship, and with him a woman, white as ice, cold as steel. To this day no one knows who she is, or what godforsaken agreement he made with them to save his life. But we soon found out what sort of a creature had come among us.'

Jessa glanced at Thorkil. He was listening intently,

his fingers working at the laces of his boots, knotting and unknotting, over and over.

'The first thing,' Mord went on, 'was that the old Jarl died one night in a storm. He was hale enough when he went to bed, but in the night he gave a sudden scream, and when they got to him he was dead. There was a mark, they say, like a spread hand, in the skin of his face; it faded away, till in the morning there was nothing left.'

Thorkil's head jerked up and his eyes met Jessa's. Mord did not notice. 'And his fingers – there was a web of ice all over them. . . . After that, it was easy. Rumours flew; fear built up. The Jarl had left no son – the Althing should have chosen another of the Wulfings, and there were plenty of good men – but they didn't. Fear made them fools. They chose Ragnar.

'Two disagreed, I remember. One was killed by a bear, the other froze in a drift on a dark night. None of his family knew why he'd left the house, but the little boy said a "white lady" had called him through the window. . . .' He looked up. 'You must have heard much of this.'

Jessa shrugged. 'Some of it. No one tells you much when you're small. But what about Kari?'

Mord glanced at the door. His voice was quiet now, barely heard. 'It happened I was with Ragnar when the news came; we were in the forest, watching them cut timber for the Hold. "A son," the messenger said, but there was something about the way he said it. Ragnar noticed too. He asked what was wrong. The man muttered something about the midwife screaming; he seemed too terrified to answer. The Jarl almost knocked me over as he rode off.

The gods help me, I've never seen a man look so stricken.'

'Did the messenger see the baby?' Jessa asked.

'No, but he didn't need to. Rumours soon got round – you know them. The child is a monster. For myself I think the High One struck at Ragnar's pride, and her sorcery. That's the god's way. They kept the child here for a while, called it Kari, but no one ever saw it except Gudrun and the old man. Ragnar has never set eyes on him.'

'So he told us,' Thorkil muttered.

'And she hates it. She'll never even hear its name – Kari. When the creature was about five years old she got Ragnar to send it away, to the ruined Hall in the North. I think she hoped it would die of cold. Brochael Gunnarsson was in prison – now he was one of the Wulfings' men, and he had said something against her, so Ragnar took his land and sent him to be the child's keeper. It was a hard revenge.' He sighed. 'I was fond of Brochael – a good man. He may be long dead. No one has been near them in all this time.'

'Until now,' Thorkil said grimly.

There was silence.

'If no one has seen him,' Jessa said suddenly, grasping at hope, 'how do they know he's so terrible?'

'Why else would she lock him up?'

It was a good answer.

'Well,' Thorkil said, 'we'll soon find out.'

Mord frowned at him. 'Be careful, lad. Be discreet. They say she can bend your mind to her will.'

Thorkil laughed coldly. 'Not mine.'

Jessa had been thinking. 'Kari and this Brochael

must be dead by now. How can they live up there?'
How will we, she thought.

'Gudrun would know. She has ways of knowing.
That's why, in these last years, your fathers and the
Wulfings stood no chance. She was too much for
them.'

Thorkil stared bleakly into the fire. Jessa pulled
absently at the ends of her hair. Mord caught his
wife's eye. 'But that's enough talk. Now we should
eat.'

The food at the Jarlshold was good and plentiful;
they had broth, and fish, and honey-cakes. Despite
her worries Jessa was hungry. What would they eat,
she wondered, at the ruined hall in the mountains?
No crops would grow there, no animals would sur-
vive. She had never known real hardship; their farm
had been a rich one. What would it be like?

When they had finished, Mord rose and pulled on
his outdoor coat. 'Come on. It's wise not keep her
waiting.'

Outside, the sky was black, frosted with stars glinting in their faint colours. The moon was a low,
silvery globe balancing, it seemed, on the very tips
of the mountains far off, lighting their frozen sum-
mits with an eerie bluish shimmer.

By now the Jarlshold was quiet, and very cold. A
few dogs loped past them as they walked between
the silent houses; once a rat ran across the frozen
mud. Like all the houses Jessa had known, these
were low and roofed with turf, boarded and shuttered now to keep the warmth of the fires in. Smoke
hung in a faint mist over the settlement.

Only the Hall was noisy; they could hear the
murmur of sound grow as they walked towards it.

The shutters were up again, but a circle of light flickered in the ring-window high up in the wall. Laughter floated out, and voices.

A doorkeeper sat outside, polishing a sword with a whetstone; a great wolf-like mastiff sprawled at his feet. Mord nodded to the man and put his hand on the latch. Then he turned. 'Don't eat anything she gives you,' he breathed. 'Don't drink. Avoid her eyes. I don't know what else to say. If she wants you – she'll get you.' Then he opened the door.

4

Never lift your eyes and look up in battle
Lest the heroes enchant you, who can change
*   warriors*
Suddenly into hogs.

It was as if some rune-master had waved a hand and
transformed the place. All the fires were lit, roaring
in the hearths, and candles and rushlights glimmered
on stands and in corners, filling the Hall with a haze
of smoke and light. Long hangings, woven of red
and green cloths, hung over the shutters, and the
trestles were scattered with scraps of food and bones
that the dogs pulled down and snarled over in the
straw. The hot air stank of smoke and spices.

Mord pushed them both forward through the
crowd. Jessa glimpsed rich embroidery on sleeves;
the glint of gold; furs; heavy pewter cups. The Jarl's
court was rich, rich on other men's land. She lifted
her chin, remembering suddenly her father's grin,
his raised hand. She had been only six when he rode
out. His face was fading from her mind.

And there was Ragnar at the high table with the
witch next to him, her face pale as a ghost's with its
long eyes, her gaze wandering the room. Grettir
sat beside her, watching Thorkil push through the
crowd.

26

Mord found them seats near one of the fires; a few men stood to make room and some of them nodded slightly at Jessa. So the Jarl still had enemies then, even here. Mord seemed uneasy; she caught him making discreet signals to someone across the room. Then a steward shouted for silence.

Noise hushed. Men settled back with full cups to see what would happen – a skald with some poem, Jessa thought, or a lawsuit, considered entertainment just as good. A tall, very thin man across the room caught her eye; he grinned at her and tugged a bundle of herbs tied with green ribbon from a bag at his feet and held it out. A pedlar. She shook her head quickly; the man laughed and winked. Then he moved out of sight among the crowd thronging the hearth.

Thorkil nudged her.

A prisoner was coming in between two of the Jarl's men. He was a tall, dark, elegant man in a dirty leather jerkin, with a gleam of gold at his neck. He looked around with cool interest.

'That's Wulfgar,' Thorkil said. 'They caught him last week up at Hagafell. He's the last of the Wulfings. If anyone should be Jarl, it's him.'

As the prisoner came through the crowd the silence grew. Jessa saw how some men looked away, but others held his eye and wished him well. He must be well liked, she thought, for them to risk even that much, with Gudrun watching.

'Wulfgar Osricsson,' Ragnar began, but the prisoner interrupted him at once. 'They all know my name, Ragnar.'

His voice was deliberately lazy. A ripple of amusement stirred in the room.

'You have plotted and warred,' Ragnar went on grimly, 'against the peace of this Hold . . .'

'My own,' Wulfgar said lightly.

'. . . and against me.'

'You! A thrall's son from Hvinir, where all they grow is sulphur and smoke-holes.'

'Be careful,' Ragnar snarled.

'Let him speak!' someone yelled from the back of the Hall. 'He has a right. Let him speak.'

Other voices joined in. The Jarl waved curtly for silence. 'He can speak. If he has anything worth hearing.'

The prisoner leaned forward and took an apple from the Jarl's table and bit into it. A guard moved, but Ragnar waved him back.

'I've nothing to say,' Wulfgar said, chewing slowly. 'Nothing that would change things. You're like a dead tree, Ragnar, smothered with a white, strangling ivy. It's poisoning you, draining you of yourself. Shake her off now, if you still can.'

Jessa, like everyone else, stared at Gudrun. She was sipping her wine and smiling. Ragnar's face flushed with rage. His reply was hoarse. 'That's enough. Rebellion means death. As you were a landed man it will be quick, with an axe. Tomorrow.'

Men in the smoky Hall looked at each other. There was a murmuring that rose to a noise. Gudrun's eyes moved across their faces as she drank.

'He can't do that!' Thorkil muttered.

Mord's hands clamped down on his shoulders and stayed there. 'Wait. Keep still.' His fingers dug into the soft coat. 'Don't draw attention to yourself.'

Wulfgar spat an apple pip on to the floor. At once, with an enormous crash, one of the shutters on the windows suddenly collapsed, flung open in a squall of wind that whipped out half the candles at a stroke. In the darkness someone yelled; Wulfgar twisted and hurled himself through the guards into the crowd of confused shadows. Strange blue smoke was billowing from the fires. Jessa coughed, half choked; in the uproar dogs were barking and Ragnar was shouting orders. Then the doors were open; men were running out among the dim houses of the Hold, letting the bitter wind stream in and slice through the smoke like a knife.

'Is he away?' Thorkil shouted, on his feet.

'He ought to be. If he was ready.'

'It was all planned. You knew!'

'Hush. Keep your voice down.'

Jessa turned; Gudrun's chair was empty. Then her eye caught sight of something lying half in the fire, smouldering; it was a small bunch of some herb, tied with a green ribbon. The stifling blue smoke was drifting from it. Jessa looked round, but the pedlar was nowhere to be seen. She bent down quickly and pulled the singed bundle out of the ashes, stamped on it and pushed it into the deep pockets of her coat, so no one saw.

'Will he really escape?' Thorkil was asking.

'If he gets out of the Hold, there's every chance. Not many who search will want to find him. He should head south, overseas.'

'And will he?'

Mord gave her a half-smile. 'I doubt it. He wants to be Jarl.' He sighed. 'There are plenty of others who want it.'

Suddenly it seemed the Hall was almost empty. Then Mord stood up. 'Ah. This is it.'

One of the Gudrun's men was beckoning them across. As they walked over, talk hushed. Jessa saw Thorkil's back stiffen.

They followed the man through a wooden archway crawling with twisted snakes. Beyond was a room lit by lamplight. Mord had to stoop under the lintel as he went in; Jessa came last, her fingers clenched tight to stop them shaking.

They were all there: Ragnar, Grettir, a few white-haired men with eyes like chips of ice – and Gudrun. Close to, she was almost beautiful. Her eyes were like water in a shallow pool, totally without colour. Cold came out of her; Jessa felt it against her face.

Outside in the Hold the search was going on; they heard running footsteps, shouts, the barking of hounds. Everywhere would be searched. Here the silence seemed intense, as if after some furious argument. Gudrun stood, watching them come; Ragnar barely turned his head. She knows, Jessa thought in a sudden panic, she knows everything. Gudrun smiled at her, a sweet, cold smile.

'The preparations for the journey are made,' Ragnar snapped. 'The ship leaves early, with the tide.' His hands tapped impatiently on the chair-arm, a smooth wolfshead, worn by many fingers.

As Gudrun moved to the table, Jessa glimpsed a peculiar glistening wisp of stuff around her wrist; she realized it was snakeskin, knotted and braided. The woman took up a jug and poured a trickle of thin red liquid into four brightly enamelled cups. Jessa picked at her glove; Thorkil's strained look caught her eye. But they would have to drink it – it was the faring-cup, always drunk before a journey. One after another, silent, they picked up the cups. Gudrun lifted hers with slim white fingers and sipped, looking at them over the rim all the while. Playing with us, Jessa thought, and drank immediately, feeling the hot sour taste flame in her throat. Thorkil tossed his off and banged the cup down empty. Mord's lips barely touched the rim.

'And we have these for you both.' She nodded to a thrall; he brought two arm-rings, thin delicate silver snakes, and gave them to Jessa and Thorkil. The silver was icy to touch; it had come from her mines where men died in the ice to find it. Jessa wanted to fling hers in the woman's face, but Mord caught her eye and she was silent, cold and stiff with anger.

Gudrun turned away. 'Take them out.'

'Wait!'

Every eye turned to Thorkil; men who had been talking fell silent. 'Don't you mind?' he asked, his fingers clenched on the ring. 'That we'll see? That we're going there . . . ?' Despite himself he could not finish.

Jessa saw a movement in the corner; it was the old man, Grettir. He had turned his head and was watching.

Gudrun stared straight at Thorkil. All she said was, 'Thrasirshall is the pit where I fling my rubbish.' She stepped close to him; he shivered in the coldness that came out from her.

'I want you to see him. I'll enjoy thinking of it. I'll enjoy watching your face, because I will see it, however far away you think me. Even in the snows and the wilderness nothing hides from me.'

She glanced down, and his eyes followed hers. He had gripped the ring so tight the serpent's mouth had cut him. One drop of blood ran down his fingers.

5

Better gear than good sense
A traveller cannot carry.

The ship lay low in the water, rocking slightly. In
the darkness it was a black shadowy mass, its dragon-
prow stark against the stars. Men, muffled into
shapelessness by heavy cloaks, tossed the last few
bundles aboard.

Jessa turned. From here the Jarlshold was a low
huddle of buildings under the hill, the Hall rising
taller than the rest, its serpent-head gables spitting
out at her.

'Did you sleep?' Thorkil asked, yawning.

'Yes.' She did not tell him about the dreams
though, the dream of walking down those endless
corridors full of closed doors; the dream of Gudrun.
Or that she had woken and opened a corner of the
shutter at midnight, gazing out into the slow, silent
snowfall, while Mord's youngest daughter had sighed
and snuggled beside her.

Now Mord was coming over, with the young man
called Helgi, who was to be captain of the ship.

'Well. . . .' Mord kissed her clumsily and thumped
Thorkil on the back. 'At least Wulfgar got away.
They won't find him now. The weather looks good
for you. . . .' For a moment he stared out over the

water. Then he said, 'Words are no use so I won't waste them. I will try and get Ragnar to revoke the exile, but he may not live long, and Gudrun will certainly not change things. You must face it. We all must.'

'We know that,' Jessa said quietly. 'Don't worry. We'll manage.'

He gazed down at her. 'I almost think you will.'

Releasing his gloved hand, she turned to the ship. As an oarsman lifted her over she saw the frosted scum of the water splinter and remake itself on the beach, and felt the splashes on her face harden and crack. The ship swayed as Thorkil sat down beside her, clumsy in his furred coat. The helmsman raised the call, and on each side sixteen oars swivelled up, white with their fur of frost. Then they dipped. At the first slap of wood in water the ship shuddered, and grated slowly off the shingle. The wharvesmen stepped back as she rocked and settled. Mord shouted, 'Good luck!'

'He's relieved to see us go,' Thorkil muttered.

'That's unfair. He's very bitter about it. Goodbye!' she yelled, leaping up, and Thorkil scrambled up into the stern and clung to the dragon's neck. 'Don't forget us, Mord! We'll be back!'

He seemed almost too far off to hear. But he nodded, bleakly. Then he turned away.

All the cold morning the ship coasted slowly down the Tarvafjord towards the open sea, carried by the icy, ebbing tide. There was little wind and the oarsmen had to row, their backs bending and knees rising in the long, silent rhythms. Fog rose from the water and froze, leaving delicate crystals of ice on spars and planks. The ship was heavy; cluttered with sea chests and baggage, casks of beer, and cargoes for the distant settlements. All around them the fog drifted, blanking out land and sky, and the only sound it did not swallow was the soft dip and splash of the oars.

Jessa and Thorkil sat huddled up in coats and blankets, slowly getting colder and stiffer. Now there seemed to be nothing to say, and nothing to do but stare out at the drifting grey air and dream and remember. Their fingers ached with cold; Jessa thought Thorkil would have been glad even to row, but no one offered him the chance. She had already noticed how the crew watched them curiously, but rarely spoke.

Gradually the fog rose. By mid-morning they could see the shore, a low rocky line, and behind it hillsides dark with trees, the snow lying among them. Once they passed a little village swathed in the smoke of its fires, but no one ran out from the houses. Only a few goats watched them glide by.

'Where are they all?' Thorkil muttered.

'Hiding.'

'From us?'

'From the Jarl. It's his ship, remember.'

At midday the sun was still low, barely above the hills. Helgi told the helmsman to put in at the next flat stretch of shore.

Slowly, the ship turned, and grazed smoothly into the shallows. As Jessa climbed out she groaned with the stiffness of her legs; the very bones of her face ached. She and Thorkil raced each other up the beach.

The oarsmen lit a fire, and handed round meat

and bread, throwing scraps on the wet shingle for the gulls to scream and fight over. Jessa noticed how Helgi kept close. Sudden running would be no use at all.

'How long will the journey take?' she asked, stretching out her legs and rubbing them.

Helgi laughed. 'Three days – longer, if the weather turns. Tonight we travel down to the sea, tomorrow up the coast to Ost, then up the Yngvir River to a village called Trond. After that – over the ice.'

Thorkil pulled a face. 'Why not go by land?'

'Because the hills are full of snow and wolves. You're anxious to arrive, are you?'

Thorkil was silenced. Looking at him, Jessa noticed the glint of silver on his arm. 'Why are you wearing that?' she asked, surprised. It was the arm-ring that Gudrun had given him.

He looked down at it, and touched the snake's smooth head. 'I don't know, I hadn't really meant to. I just put it on. . . . It's valuable, after all. Where's yours?'

'In the baggage, but I've a good mind to throw it over the side. It's bad luck. I don't know how you can wear it.'

Thorkil scowled. 'I will if I want. It's mine.'

Jessa shook her head. 'It's hers,' she said, thinking how vain he was.

'Well, don't throw yours in the sea,' Helgi laughed. 'Throw it to me instead. The sea is rich enough.'

'I might.'

Thorkil looked up suddenly. 'Your men. Are they coming with us all the way?'

'To the very door,' Helgi said grimly. Behind him

35

the oarsmen's talk faltered, as if they had listened for his answer.

The ship reached the coast late that evening, the watchman of Tarva challenging them suddenly out of the darkness, his voice ringing across the black water. Jolted awake, Jessa heard the helmsman yell an answer, and saw the lights of the settlement ripple under the bows as the ship edged in among the low wharves.

They spent that night in the house of a merchant named Savik, who knew Helgi well, warm in his hall with three oarsmen sprawling and dicing near the only doorway. Where the rest went to, Jessa did not ask. She managed a brief word with Thorkil at the table.

'No chances yet.'

He threw her a troubled look. 'You heard what he said. We won't have any chances.'

'Yes, but keep your eyes open. You never know.'

'I suppose we could always jump overboard,' he said savagely.

Later, she slept fitfully. In her sleep she felt the rocking of the boat, as if it still carried her down the long, icy fjord, and there at the end of it, floating on the sea, was a great, dark building, the winds howling in its empty passages like wolves.

In the morning they left early as the wind was good, and as soon as they reached open water the sail was dropped with a flapping of furled canvas and the slap of ropes – a single rectangular sheet woven of strong striped cloth. The wind plumped it out into a straining arc; the ship shuddered and plunged through the spray. Jessa climbed up into the prow and watched

the white sea birds wheel overhead and scream in
the cliffs and crannies. Seals bobbed their heads out
and watched her with dark, intelligent eyes; in bays
their sluggish shining bodies lay like great pebbles
on the shingle.

She turned to the oarsmen squatting in the bottom
of the boat out of the wind; some sleeping, others
gaming with dice for brooches or metal rings –
Thorkil with them, and losing badly, it seemed.

After a while Helgi clambered over and sat beside
her.

'Do you feel well? No sickness?'

'Not yet.'

He grinned. 'Yes, it may well come. But we have
to put off some cargo at Wormshold this afternoon –
that will give you a chance to go ashore. It's a big,
busy settlement, under the Worm's Head.'

'Worm's Head?'

'Yes. Never seen it? I'll show you.' He took out
a knife and scratched a few lines into the wooden
prow. 'It's a spit of land, look, that juts out into the
sea. Like this. It looks like a dragon's head, very
rough and rocky – a great hazard. There are small
islets here, and skerries at the tip. The Flames, we
call them. The currents are fierce around them. That
dragon's eaten many a good ship. But you'll see it
soon.'

And she did, as the ship flew through the morning.
At first a grey smudge on the sea; then a rocky
shape, growing as they sped towards it into a huge
dragon's head and neck of stone, stretched out chin-
deep in the grey waves, its mouth wide in a snarl,
dark hollows and caves marking nostrils and eyes.
The wind howled as they sailed in under it, the

swell crashing and sucking and booming deep in the gashed, treacherous rocks.

Wormshold was squeezed into a small haven in the dragon's neck. As soon as Jessa saw it, she knew this would be their chance, perhaps their only chance. It was a busy trading place, full of ships, merchants, fishermen, pedlars, skalds, thieves and travelling fraudsters of every kind. Booths and trestle tables full of merchandise crowded the waterfront; the stink of fish and meat and spices hung over the boats.

Here they could be lost, quickly and easily; she had coins sewn into the hems of her skirts; help could be bought. She tried to catch Thorkil's eyes, but he seemed silent and depressed.

'It'll never work,' he said.

'What's the matter with you! We can try, can't we!' He nodded, unconvinced.

They wandered stiffly about, glad to walk and run, even though two of Helgi's men, the one called Thrand and the big noisy one, Steinar, trailed around behind them. Jessa felt excitement pulse through her. Only two. It might have been much worse.

They stared at the goods for sale. Strange stuff, most of it, from the warmer lands to the south: wrinkled fruits, fabrics in bales and bolts, shawls, belts, buckles, fine woollen cloaks flapping in the sea wind. Rows of stiff hides creaked and swung; there were furs, coloured beads, bangles and trinkets of amber and whalebone and jet. One booth sold only rings, hundreds of them strung in rows, rings for fingers, neck, arms, of all metals, chased or plain or intricately engraved.

With a word to Steinar, Thrand stepped into the

crowd, pushing his way to a man sharpening knives. Jessa saw him pull his own out and hand it over. So that left one.

She bought some sweetmeats from a farmwife and she and Thorkil ate them, watching a blacksmith hammer out a spearhead and plunge it with a hiss into a bucket of water. As Thorkil fingered the hanging weapons enviously, someone jolted gently against Jessa's shoulder.

'A thousand apologies,' murmured a low voice.

A thin, lanky man stood beside her, his coat patched and ragged. He winked slyly. Astonished, she stared at him, then glanced carefully round. Steinar was a good way back, trying to buy ale.

'You travel fast down the whale's road,' the pedlar said quietly, examining a brooch on a stall.

'So do you,' Jessa gasped. 'Where is Wulfgar? Is he with you?'

'That outlaw?' He grinned at her. 'That prince of the torn coat? What makes you think I would know?'

She took the fragments of herbs out of her pocket and rubbed them thoughtfully between her fingers, until their faint scent reached him.

'These.'

The pedlar glanced at them quickly and made a soundless whistle. 'Well. You have very good eyes. As for Wulfgar, people are saying he's fled south. They may be right.'

'That's not what I think.' She watched Thorkil weighing a sword in his hand. Then she said, 'Others might want to escape. This might be a good time.'

The pedlar dropped the brooch and picked up another; his eyes swept the crowd with a swift glance.

'I had heard where they were sending you. But the snake-woman has eyes that see too far.'

She stared at him angrily. 'If you won't help, I'll try anyway. I don't want to spend the rest of my life starving in Thrasirshall with – whatever's there. I can pay you, if that's what you want.'

He put the brooch down and turned to her.

'I thought you were braver.'

'Only about some things.'

'Then listen.' His voice was suddenly sharp and urgent. 'Don't do anything. Trust me. You must wait until you hear from me, no matter how long it takes. *Don't* try to escape. Promise!'

'But . . .'

'Promise! I won't let you down.'

She gave a sigh of bewilderment. 'All right. But we leave here soon!'

'It won't be here. Don't worry. When you see me again, you'll understand everything.'

As she stared at him she saw the man Steinar push nearer.

'I'm afraid not,' she said loudly. 'It's too expensive.'

'Ah, lady,' the pedlar said at once, scratching his cheek, 'please yourself. Next time I'll bring you better goods. Trust me.'

With a wink he turned away in the crowd.

Thorkil touched her arm. 'There you are. Steinar's coming. He's had too much to drink, by the look of him.'

'Rubbish.' The man was behind them; his breath stank of beer. One heavy hairy hand clamped down on Thorkil's shoulder. 'Back to the ship.'

Helgi was waiting for them, rather anxiously. He

gave Steinar a few sharp words but the man just shrugged and sprawled into his place among the oarsmen. Thrand came late, cursed by everyone.

The men rowed out into the current. The wind was freshening and the sea seemed much rougher; white flecks topped the waves.

Looking back, Jessa saw no sign of the pedlar. She leaned her chin on her hands, thoughtfully. She had promised to wait, and she would, but she couldn't help feeling they'd missed their chance. Now every day took them nearer to Thrasirshall. But there had been something in the man's look that had comforted her; some hidden spark of knowledge and, yes, laughter. He'd been laughing at her. He knew something that she didn't, that was why.

6

Short are the sails of a ship,
Dangerous the dark . . .

By late afternoon the storm was on them. Icy rain
pelted down, hurled like glinting spears into eyes
and faces. Jessa was already drenched, although she
and Thorkil sat in the bottom of the boat with a sheet
of sailcloth around them. When the water began to
lap their ankles they had to move and help bail. The
ship rose and fell, toppling into enormous troughs,
buffeted by waves that curled high over the deck.
Through the spasms of rain and hail, Jessa could
barely see the oarsmen clenched over their oars, or
Helgi, hanging half out of the prow, dripping with
spray, yelling when they swerved too near the rocks.
The iron-grey cliffs hung over them, the boat crashed
and rose through the floundering seas, every spar
and timber straining and shrieking. Sick and numb,
Jessa flung water over the side. Time had gone; she
had been doing this for ever. Cold nailed her feet to
the deck, every bone ached, the world rose and fell
and floundered around her.

As darkness fell, the rain froze into masses of ice
on the timbers, so that they had to hack it off with
knives and fling it overboard. Once Helgi gave a
great yell; the helmsman jerked the rudder and the

ship skimmed a bank of shingle, grating horribly, flinging them all down. Then the wind came about, and hauled the ship into a trough, and out, swinging her round. Staggering up, Jessa saw that they had cleared the headland; the rain drove now from an empty sky.

Night thickened quickly. Shields and baggage and casks of beer were flung out into the black hollows. Jessa's eyes were stinging with the salt and hail that bounced from the deck; her arms ached, frozen to her sleeves, and however hard she bailed, the water still rose, lapping the ankles of the oarsmen, who spat out curses and sardonic remarks.

At last, exhausted, she sank back on her heels, clinging to the rail. The storm roared around her; she heard strange wailings in the sea, voices on the wind, screaming, whispering spells, spinning the boat with their breath. Closing her eyes she saw Wulfgar standing in the Hall; the hangings of the Jarlshold flapped; something walked and padded on strange feet through corridors and locked rooms, a creature with Gudrun's eyes that held out a thin silver arm-ring, pressing it into her hands. She could feel it; she had it out of the bag where it had been hidden. It seemed to her that she turned to the sea, opened her numb fingers, and let the weight of it, the enormous weight, slide swiftly over the side. Then she lay down among the wet baggage. She was asleep when Helgi saw the harbour fire at Ost.

In the morning, she wondered what was real and what was dream. Ost was a filthy place; a squalid mess of huts and muddy pens, the people shifty-eyed and half starved. Behind the settlement, the

43

mountains with their ice-white cliffs plunged straight down into the fjord; the pastures were icebound most of the year, the animals lean and hollow-eyed. The chieftain was a small greasy man who called Helgi 'Sir' and Thorkil and herself 'Lord' and 'Lady', his greedy eyes always on their cloaks and amulets. Helgi stayed with them all the time, and the oarsmen kept together, starting no fights and wearing their weapons conspicuously. The Jarl's hold on the land was weakening as they travelled north; they were coming to wild country full of outlaws and hunted men.

As the ship was being repaired, Jessa rummaged through her bag.

'What are you looking for?' She hadn't heard Thorkil climb aboard behind her. He looked tired, and the fine stitchery of his coat was already soiled and stained.

She closed the bag up. 'The arm-ring. Gudrun's. It's not here.'

'Do you mean it's been stolen?'

'No.' Jessa shrugged and half laughed. 'I think I threw it over the side after all. Last night. I suppose I must have been half asleep.'

He glared at her angrily. 'Jessa, that was silver! We could have found a use for it!'

She shrugged. 'I'm glad to get rid of it. I hardly thought I'd ever see you wearing her favours either. Are you going to sell yours then?'

His fingers ran over the smooth silver head.

'Not yet.'

'You're keeping it?'

'For now. It does no harm, does it?'

'I suppose not,' she said uneasily. But she didn't tell him about the pedlar, as she had meant to.

They were glad to leave Ost, but as they entered the fjord and turned inland, the menace of Thrasirshall was creeping nearer. And still the pedlar had not appeared. Jessa tried not to think about him. What if he had been in Gudrun's pay, and tricked her? She was furious with herself.

All morning they rowed up the still water, watching the jagged cliffs rise up on each side, scraped sheer by the retreating glacier.

Thorkil sat silent, fingering his arm-ring. The men too were morose and watchful; they only spoke in mutters. Helgi stood in the prow, his hand rubbing the great dragon's neck, rarely turning his head. Silent and ominous, the narrow craft slid into the harbour of Trond at noon.

The place seemed deserted. A few boats were dragged up on the shingle. Wisps of smoke drifted from the small turf houses, their roofs green with grass. Helgi climbed out and waited. Finally he called out. No one answered. Jessa could hear the faint lap of the tidal water against the boat; skuas and gulls screamed in the crags.

Then a dog barked, and a tall man stepped up on to a rock above them, a long fishing spear glinting in his hand.

'What's your business?' he asked, after a long stare.

'Messengers,' Helgi said curtly. 'From the Jarl Ragnar.'

'To us?'

Helgi hesitated. Then he said, 'To Thrasirshall.'

It must have been a great shock, but the man barely showed it. 'Can you prove that?'

Helgi took the Jarl's token from his pocket – a ring, in silver, marked with one rune – and flung it up. The man caught it, and looked at it carefully. Then his eyes moved over the ship. Jessa heard the whisper of a sword slowly unsheathing behind her.

'Keep that still!' Helgi hissed without turning.

Quickly the man scrambled down the rocks, soil and pebbles slithering away under his feet. When he was quite near them he stood still. He was a tall, grey man, with a weathered face. 'I'm not alone. There are many of us, as you'll guess, so I advise you, friend with the sword, to hold your hand. Your token, master.'

The silver ring was dropped into Helgi's hand. Steinar slammed his sword back in its sheath.

'Now,' the man said, 'what do you want from us?' There was a change in his voice; Helgi heard it too, and gave a wry smile. 'Your hospitality, chieftain, for a few nights. Also safe haven for the ship and the men left with her. Most important, sledges, dogs, and if you have them, horses for those of us going on to the Hall. This will all be paid for on our return.'

'Your return!' The man raised an eyebrow. 'Master, you'll pay for it before you go. No one takes that road and returns.'

Suddenly he turned and shouted. Men seemed to spring up, a silent crop from the rocks. There were some young lads, but most were older like their leader; hard, coarse-looking men, but strong, and probably handy, Jessa thought, with those axes and spears. They came down and stared at the strangers, especially Jessa and Thorkil. A few women leaned in the doors of the houses.

'Come with me.' The tall man led Jessa, Thorkil and Helgi to a small hall, warm and dark inside, with a good fire blazing in the hearth.

'Now,' he said, sitting down. 'Dogs and sleds we have aplenty, but the way you wish to take is far too treacherous for sleds. You'll need horses. And those are precious, this far north.'

'But you have them?'

'For the right price.' As he spoke, a few other men came in. Warmed wine was served out by a thin woman with untidy hair. Jessa sipped hers thankfully.

'My name is Sigmund – they call me Greycloak,' the man added.

'You are the chieftain?'

The man looked at him over his cup. 'Indeed no. We have no chieftains here, master; no one man better than the others. I am elected to speak. We still do that here.'

Helgi frowned. 'The Jarl . . .'

'Did I mention the Jarl?' Sigmund said at once, looking round with pretended surprise. The other men laughed.

Helgi looked uneasy. 'What price, then, for these horses?'

'First, my duty as a host. This young lady must be looked after.'

He called one of the girls over and spoke to her quietly. Then she came up to Jessa. 'Come with me,' she said, with a shy smile.

As she followed, Jessa saw Helgi's anxious look,

and grinned at him. Then the door closed between them.

Warm water was wonderful, after so long without it, and clean clothes made her feel ten times better. The girl looked on curiously, fingering a brooch.

'This is nice. Did you get it at the Jarlshold?'

'No.'

'Is the Jarlshold splendid? And the Snow-walker, Gudrun, is she as evil as they say?'

'Yes she is,' Jessa said absently as she laced her boots. 'She's also very powerful. I'd be careful what you say, even here.'

'Oh, we are protected from her here.'

Jessa looked up. 'Protected?'

'Yes.' The girl came and sat next to her, on a bright tapestry stool. Her fingers picked absently at the stitches. 'We knew you were coming.'

Jessa was astonished. Then she thought of the pedlar.

'How did you know?'

'Through the runes. And my father has given me a message for you. If you are really prisoners of those men, you and the boy, then you must tell me. We will release you.'

Jessa's mind was working quickly. 'Has the pedlar arranged this?'

The girl looked puzzled. 'What pedlar?'

'Never mind. . . . How could you release us?'

'The crew would be killed. No one would be surprised if they never went back. Longships are often lost in storms. And no news ever comes out of Thrasirshall. The Jarl would never know if you'd got there or not.'

It was all so sudden. Jessa thought for a while.

48

The pedlar could never have got here before them. And if these people knew 'by the runes', that meant sorcery.

'How do we know it's not a trap?' she said at last. 'Why help us?'

The girl shrugged. 'Because of your father.'

Jessa got up and wandered over to the fire. So that was it. They were Wulfings' men. She thought about the promise she had made the pedlar – that stupid promise! – and then about the black, monstrous building somewhere far out there in the snow. Not to have to go there, all that long journey. But he had seemed so sure. And Gudrun — would she really be fooled?

'What do you mean, that you're protected here?' She turned quickly. 'What protects you? Is it sorcery?'

The girl's black eyes looked up at her. 'The shamanka does it. When Gudrun looks at us here, she sees only mist. The shamanka knew you were coming.'

'Can I speak to her?'

The girl thought, then nodded. 'Very well. Tonight. I'll arrange it.'

'Good. And tell your father' – she paused – 'that I thank him, but he must do nothing. Not yet.'

Again, the girl nodded.

'And you can keep the brooch too,' Jessa said, 'if you like.'

7

Now is answered what you ask of the runes.

Jessa woke suddenly, her eyes wide. In the darkness someone was crouching next to her; a hand was gripping her shoulder tight.

'Come with me,' the girl's voice whispered in her ear.

With a sigh, Jessa heaved off the warm covers, slipped on her coat and soft leather boots. Then she followed, silently, through the swinging curtain of the booth.

It was dark in the hall, and smelt of ale and meat. The fire had smouldered low, and some of the oarsmen lying in the corners snored. Carefully, the girls slipped between them. One dog raised its head and watched. As they passed Thorkil's booth Jessa paused, but the girl shook her head. 'Only you. No one else.'

At the door Helgi's guard was breathing heavily, slumped against the wall. All at once Jessa realized that the men had been drugged – no trained warrior would sleep as heavily as this. She stepped over him thoughtfully.

Outside, the world was black. Water lapped against the shingle far off, and up on a hill a breeze rustled stiff branches. The girl led Jessa between the houses to one by itself at the edge of the settlement, and as they walked their feet splintered the puddles on the open ground. Above them, the sky suddenly rippled and broke into light. Looking up, Jessa saw the eerie flicker of the aurora above the trees; a green and gold and blue haze over the stars, its gauzy shape flowing and rippling like a curtain.

'Surt's blaze,' the girl remarked. 'The poets would say they were feasting in Gianthome.'

Jessa nodded, caught in the strange light that made the snow glimmer. Then she ducked her head and followed the girl into the low doorway.

Inside, it was dim and smoky; at the far end she could see someone sitting over the fire. She fumbled forward slowly, and sat on an empty stool. The room was stiflingly warm; around her the walls were hung with thick tapestries, dim woven webs of gods and giants, trolls and strange creatures.

Opposite her sat an aged woman, her face wizened and yellow. Her thin hair was braided into intricate knots and plaits; amulets and luckstones were hung and threaded among her clothes. She wore a stiff cloak sewn with birds' feathers, glossy in the dimness. As Jessa watched, the old woman's hand, its skin dried tight over the knuckles, drifted among the stones on the table in front of her, moving one, turning another over – small, flat pebbles, each marked with its own black rune.

'Wait outside, Hana.'

The curtain flickered as the girl moved through it.

Jessa waited, watching the hands turn the worn pebbles. Then, without lifting her eyes, the woman said, 'It is not that I have her powers. You must know that. I do not know what sort of a creature she is, this Gudrun No-onesdaughter, or what gods she worships, but she is strong. Still' – and a pebble clicked in the dimness – 'I have something, some slight skill, gathered over the years. I have spread my mind like a bird's wing over this kin. Here, we are safe. She cannot see us.'

'Then if we were to stay here – Thorkil and I . . .'

'She would not know of it. But you would not be able to leave. Her mind is the surface of a lake – all the world's reflections move across it.'

Jessa edged away from the fire, which was scorching her knees.

'Yes, but escape . . . it would mean the men would be killed?'

'Men!' The old woman looked up; her mouth twisted in a grim smile. 'What are men? There are plenty more.'

Chilled, Jessa was silent a moment. Then she said quietly, 'I won't have them killed. I won't have that.'

The pebbles turned. 'There is no other way. They cannot go back – she would make them speak.'

'That's it then. We must just go on.' She said it as firmly as she could. Only her word was keeping a dagger out of Helgi's ribs, yes, and the others too. And this wasn't the way.

The old woman turned a last pebble and gazed down at it. 'So the runes tell me.'

Jessa edged forward. The room seemed darker; something rustled behind her. The old woman's amulets clicked as she moved.

'Do you know,' Jessa whispered, 'what lives in Thrasirshall? Is there anything there still alive?'

'There is fear there. Yours. Your cousin's. Gudrun's.'

'Hers?'

The woman chuckled. 'Oh, hers above' all. Her eyes are always this way. Nine years ago Brochael Gunnarsson landed here. There was one with him, so muffled in coats and furs against the ice that no one could see him. So it has always been. They went north; they have not been heard of since. But I have felt her thought stretching out like a hand, touching, jerking back. Oh yes, there is something in the Hall, something alive, and she fears it, as she fears her mirror.'

Jessa touched one of the stones. It was cool and smooth. 'What do you mean, her mirror?'

'Gudrun never looks in a glass.' The shamanka turned and spat into the fire. 'The runes have said her own reflection will destroy her. There are no mirrors in the Jarlshold.'

And then with a rustle of feathers the old woman reached out and caught Jessa's wrist – a tight, cold grip. 'One thing. She will have not let you go without some link, some tie to bind you to her. Find it. Break it. Whatever it costs you.'

'As for Kari Ragnarsson . . . sometimes, in the darkest part of the night, I have thought that I felt . . . something. A cold, strange touch on my mind.' She shrugged and sat back, gazing at Jessa. 'But I do not know what he is. When you find out, you might come and tell me.'

The road was an ancient one, built by giants. No one used it now – after only a few miles it dwindled into a frozen track wandering through the boulders and scree of the fjordshore. The six horses and the pack-mule picked their way along it, sometimes

53

sinking fetlock-deep in the icy bog. Jessa was stiff from jerking forward to keep her balance.

They were already four hours out from Trond, the wind howling at them down ravines in the steep rock face. They had started before dawn, but even now it was barely light enough to make out the track as it began to turn inland, towards the hills. Muffled in cloaks and coats, only their eyes visible, the riders had spread out in a straggling line, urging on their slithering, nervous horses. Helgi went first, with Thorkil and Jessa close behind him. Then came the three men who had drawn the marked stones out of Helgi's glove at Trond, when the oarsmen had argued about who was to go further. Thorgard Blund, and his cousin, the thin man called Thrand, and the big, loud-mouthed Steinar, called Hairy-hand. Jessa wondered how they felt now; there had been some bitter words back there. Now the three kept together, watchful and resentful.

The track climbed up, moving slowly above the snowline. Now the horses strode in each other's hoof-holes across a great snowfield, dazzlingly white, broken only by streams that gurgled under their seamed, frozen lids. These were invisible, and treacherous; once Thorkil's horse lurched forward into one, almost throwing him. After that they kept direction only by the sun, but the sky slowly clouded over. By late afternoon they had lost the track altogether.

Finally Helgi stopped, and swore. The narrow valley down which they had come was closed by a sheer rock face, glistening with icicles and glassy twists of frozen water. He turned. 'We'll have to go back. This isn't it.'

Jessa saw Steinar glance at his colleagues. 'What about a rest?' he growled. 'The horses need it.'

Helgi looked at Jessa. She tugged the frosted scarf from her mouth. 'I'm in no hurry.'

They found an overhang of cliff and sat under it; Helgi fed the horses, then he joined them. They ate slowly, listening to the bleak wind in the hollow rocks. The other three sat apart, talking in gruff, quiet voices. Helgi watched them; finally they called him over, and when he came they stood up. Steinar was bigger and heavier than the younger man. He put his hand on Helgi's shoulder. Talk became hurried, noisy, almost an argument.

'I don't like the look of that,' Thorkil muttered.

Jessa raised her eyes from a daydream. Helgi was shaking his head angrily. He snapped something sharp and final.

'They're scared,' Thorkil said. 'They don't want to go on.'

'I don't blame them.'

They watched the bitter, hissed argument. These were soldiers, Jessa thought, trained how to fight, to deal with things, but how could they deal with this? The horror of whatever was in Thrasirshall had caught hold of them; it was wearing at their nerves.

'Do you think he'll make them go on?'

'He'll try. But it's three to one.'

'Three to three.'

Thorkil flashed her a brief grin. 'You're right. But remember, if we were . . . out of the way, they wouldn't have to go on at all. They've probably been thinking about that.'

Helgi flung Steinar's hand from him and turned

55

away. He marched past Jessa and caught the horse's bridle.

'Ride close to me,' he muttered. 'And pray we find the place soon.'

8

A wayfarer should not walk unarmed,
But have his weapons to hand:
He knows not when he may need a spear,
Or what menace meet on the road.

It was a hard thing to pray for. Jessa swung on to
her weary horse and gathered up the reins, moving
out hurriedly after Thorkil. Looking back, she saw
that Steinar and Thorgard Blund were still listening
to the thin man, Thrand. His voice was a quiet echo
under the cliff. Steinar laughed, and turned, catching
her eye. He put his huge hands up to his horse and
hauled himself up.

Jessa and Thorkil rode close together. Neither
spoke. The path ran along the edge of a vast pinewood, its branches still and heavy with snow. In
there it was dim and gloomy, the trees receding into
endless aisles, only a few birds piping in the hush.
Once a pine marten streaked across the track.

Helgi was guessing the way now, and they all knew
it. The sun became a cold blue globe, sliding down
into mists and vapours; twilight turned the world
black and grey. The snow lost its glare and shim-
mered blue; crystals of ice hardened on the tree-
trunks.

Without turning his head, Helgi muttered, 'Thorkil. Can you use that knife of yours?'

'What knife?'

'The sharp one you've been keeping under your coat.'

Thorkil grinned. 'It's not the only thing that's sharp. Yes, I can use it.'

Jessa glanced back. Three wraiths on shadow-horses flickered through the trees. 'Listen, Helgi . . .'

'Don't worry. It may not come to that. It wouldn't help us if it does.' His eyes moved anxiously over the dark fells. 'I'd be glad to see that hell-hole now, troll or no troll.'

Silence, except for the swish of snow. Jessa loosened the blade in her belt, warm under her coat. Night fell on them, like a great bird; the stars glittered through the trees. She thought of the pedlar, his urgent voice saying, 'Wait for me.' But where was he? He had abandoned them.

Then the voice came from behind.

'Captain!'

With a clink of harness, Helgi drew his horse to a halt. He sat still a moment, his back rigid. Then he turned round.

The three horsemen waited in a line. Their swords gleamed in the starlight. Ice glinted on their clothes and beards.

'We've come far enough,' Steinar said. 'We're going back.'

'Go then. I should have brought braver men.'

The man laughed. 'What's courage against trolls and monsters? Come back with us, man.'

'What will you tell the Jarl?' Helgi asked, his voice clear across the frost. 'And what will you say to *her*?'

Steinar glanced at Thrand.

'My father was a poet,' the thin man remarked. 'I can feel a story coming to me too. It concerns two children who fell overboard in a storm.'

With a slither of sound Helgi drew his sword. 'Not while I'm alive.'

Suddenly, the pack-mule jerked. A black shape flapped down through the branches, dusting snow into Jessa's hair, and another followed it; two enormous, glossy ravens, that clung and settled on the bouncing branches.

Helgi laughed grimly, his hand tight on his horse's mane. 'Look at that. The High One has two birds like that. He sends them out to see everything that happens in the world. My job is to take these two to Thrasirshall and keep them safe on the way. If you're coming, come. Otherwise go back. But don't think I'll keep your cowardice quiet.'

Steinar's harness creaked as he moved forward. 'It's a waste, lad. Though I suppose the wolves won't think so.'

The ravens karked. Snow swirled in the darkness. 'Better ride, Jessa,' Helgi growled, but she was ready; she dug her heels in and the horse leapt forward into a sky that tore itself apart in front of her. The aurora crackled into a great arch of green fire and scarlet flame; Jessa thundered into it over the hard snow, could feel the eerie light tingling on her face. Branches loomed at her and she ducked, lying low and breathless on the warm, sweating skin of the horse. Voices yelled; Thorkil shouted; something whistled over her head and thudded into the snow.

59

She kicked hard; the horse burst through the edge of the wood, leapt a black stream hanging rigid on its stones, and began to flounder up the white sides of the fell. The sky crackled and spat light; her horse was green, then gold, then scarlet. Behind her Thorkil galloped, coat flapping, his face shimmering with colours. Up and up through the deep snow, kicking the horse, urging it, swearing at it, and then, at last, the top!

She came over the lip of the white hill through the stars and an arch of flame. A great wind roared in her ears; the horse stood, snorting clouds of breath.

'Go on!' Thorkil was yelling. 'Don't stop now!' His own horse fought and floundered up the slope.

But Jessa did not move. She sat, looking ahead, her hair whipping out in the gale.

'There's nowhere left to go,' she called grimly.

Beside her, he gazed breathlessly down into the valley.

At Thrasirshall.

It was huge even from here: a mass of black, broken towers hung with ice. The aurora flickered silently over it, tingeing glassy walls, dark window-slits. A thin moon balanced on the hills behind, its light piercing the shattered roofs, stretching the Hall's long shadow over the blue unbroken snow.

No smoke rose from the roofs; no animals lowed in the byres. It was a silent ruin.

Jessa heard Helgi's horse snort behind her, and then the other three come to a slow, doubtful stop. She didn't move, or care. All the danger from behind had gone. It had been sucked down into that black, glittering ruin below them.

After a long silence Thorkil said, 'It's empty.

There are no lights, no tracks in the snow. They must be dead long since.'

'Maybe.' Helgi turned his head, the colours of Surt's blaze flickering on his face. 'Well?' he said quietly.

The three men were staring at the Hall, their horses fidgeting uneasily. Then Steinar sheathed his sword with a snap. He glanced at the others; Thrand shrugged.

'We should keep together.' They seemed to have lost all will; Jessa saw how their eyes kept straying to the tower.

'Nothing will be said?'

'Nothing.' Helgi's voice was rich with contempt. Without another word he turned his horse and moved forward. The howl of a wolf broke out in the wood behind them; then another answered, not so far away. The horses flicked their ears nervously.

The riders moved together in a tight knot, down the long white slope of the hill. No one spoke. Behind them the pack-mule floundered, its rope slack.

As they came down to the ruin, they could hear the wind moaning through the broken walls. The snow down here had drifted into great banks; they pushed cautiously through it, into the shadow of the walls. At the first archway, its keystone hanging dangerously low, they halted.

'Torches,' Thrand muttered. 'The more light the better.'

Helgi nodded. The gaunt stones beside him were coated in ice; frozen in smooth lumps and layers. Nothing moved.

They had brought torches of pitch from the boat.

It took an age to make flame, but then the soaked wood flared and crackled, making the horses start in the acrid smoke. 'Two will be enough,' Helgi said, bending and picking one up. 'I'll go first. You, Steinar, at the back. Take the other light with you.'

They moved through the arch. Its gates were long gone, rotted to one black post that stuck out of the snow like a burnt finger. Torchlight gleamed on frozen stone, on shapeless masses of ice that might once have been carvings. As they came to the inner gate they saw it was blocked; a row of long smooth icicles of enormous thickness hung down to the ground. Helgi and Thrand had to dismount and hack at them with sword and flame; each snapped with a great crack that rang in the ruins.

One by one, the horses squeezed through. Now they found themselves in a courtyard, a great square of white. Winds and breezes moaned in the outbuildings, sounding like voices, creaking a timber door somewhere out of sight, gusting snow from the sills of windows high in the Hall. The silence held them still; the silence and the emptiness. Kari is dead, Jessa thought. Whatever he was.

Helgi turned. 'There's a door there, look. We might be able to get inside.'

He dismounted and waded over, knee-deep in snow. As he held the torch up, the flames lit the door; it was made of ancient wood, studded with nails, and had once been repaired with planks hammered over the weak places, but even these were now green with rot. Helgi kicked it; it shuddered but held. In the darkening air they waited, stiff with fear, but there was no sound or stir from within.

Helgi drew his knife. At the same time something

62

black screeched from the sky. Helgi yelled with fright and dropped the torch; the horses reared and plunged. In sudden blackness dim shadows flapped overhead.

Jessa shrieked. Someone caught her arm.

'Quiet! Helgi?'

Steinar had pushed forward, torch in hand. In the red light they saw Helgi scramble from his knees, his face white. 'I'm all right.'

'What was it?'

He looked up. 'Birds. Two of them.'

They were perched on the sill above him; the two ravens from the wood. Their eyes followed every movement.

Steinar gripped the thorshammer at his neck. 'This is a place of sorcery, or worse. Let's get out, man. While we can!'

But Helgi snatched the torch from his hand and turned, holding it up. Then he stopped, stock-still.

Jessa's fingers clenched on the frozen reins.

Before them, the door was opening.

It was tugged open, jerking and grating against the stones as if the wood was swollen.

Firelight streamed out, as if a slot had opened in a dark lantern. It fell on their faces, glinted in the horses' eyes. A scatter of snow falling through it turned red as blood.

A man stood there. He was a giant; his head reached the lintel of the door, and though he was so wrapped in furs and patched cloaks they saw his strength. His face was flushed with the fire's heat; his beard and hair dark red, cut close.

Helgi gripped his knife, looking suddenly small and pale on the cold steps. The big man gave him a glance, then pushed him aside and shouldered his way down among the horses. He came straight to Jessa. She could feel the warmth of the fire glowing from him as he gripped her horse's mane.

'You're late, Jessa,' he said. 'A good soup is almost spoiled.'

9

Greetings to the host. The guest has arrived.
In which seat shall he sit?

The chair was too big for her, and had once been covered with some embroidery; the firelight glimmered on a patch of trees and a threadbare reindeer. She snuggled back and sipped the soup. It was so hot it scorched her tongue.

They were in a small room, very dark. There was another ragged chair, a table, and in a corner some empty shelves, their shadows jerking in the firelight. By the hearth a stack of cut logs oozed dampness. The window was boarded up, and some torn shreds of green cloth were nailed across it to keep out draughts.

Jessa's knees were hot; she edged back. Her coat was dripping into a puddle on the floor.

On the table lay two fishing spears and a knife, thrust deep into the timber. Thorkil was trying to pull it out, but couldn't.

'That's another thing,' he said, tapping the empty platter. 'Enough food for six. Everything prepared. How did he know?'

She shook her head.

Outside, voices approached, the door shuddered open. The big man, Brochael, came in, and Helgi trailed behind him, glancing quickly into the shadows. They had all done that. No one forgot that the creature was here, somewhere.

'We're going, Jessa,' Helgi said quickly.

She stared at him. 'Tonight?'

He shrugged, unhappily. 'You've seen. They won't stay here. To be frank, neither will I. There's too much strangeness in this place.' She nodded, wordless.

'I'm just sorry to have to leave you both here.'

'Don't be.' Brochael planted himself in front of the blaze. 'They'll be safer here than in any hold of Gudrun's.'

Helgi gave her a wan smile and went to the door. Suddenly Jessa wanted to go with him; she leapt up, spilling the soup, but he caught her eye and she stopped.

'Good luck,' he said. Then he went out and closed the door.

In the sudden silence they heard the clink of harness, the muffled scrape of a hoof in snow. After that there was only the wind, howling over the sills and under the doors into all the empty rooms and spaces of the Hall.

Brochael sat down. He cleared the table with one sweep of his arm, tugged out the knife and thrust it in his belt, and leaned both elbows on the bare wood. 'Now. I already know your names and I'm sure you can guess mine. I am Brochael Gunnarsson, of Hartfell. I knew your fathers, a long time ago. I also know that Ragnar has sent you here into exile.'

'How do you know?' Jessa demanded. 'How could you?'

Brochael took down a candle and lit it. 'I was

told,' he said. There was something in his voice that puzzled her, but she was too tired to think about it now.

She took the letter out of her inner pocket and held it out.

'Were you told about this?'

He took it, looked at her a moment, then put the candle down and tugged open the knots that held the sealskin. A square of parchment fell out; he unfolded it on the table, spreading it flat with his big hands.

They all leaned over it. Spindly brown letters were marked on the rough vellum. Bochael fingered them. 'It's brief enough.'

He read it aloud. 'From Ragnar, Jarl, to Brochael Gunnarsson, this warning. When I die she will come for the creature. It may be to kill, or it may be for some reason of her own. Take him south, out of these lands. I would not have him suffer as I have suffered.'

There was silence. Then Brochael folded the parchment. 'Does he think I don't know,' he said roughly. He picked up the candle.

'Come with me' he said. 'All this gossip can wait until morning.'

He led them to a thick curtain in one corner, and pulled it back. Beyond it was the usual sleeping-booth – it was well panelled in wood, the blankets patched and coarse. 'The other is next to it.' Brochael put the candle down. 'Not the silks of the Jarlshold, but just as warm. Sleep well, for as long as you like. We'll talk tomorrow.'

'Where do you sleep?' Thorkil asked, looking at the damp blanket with obvious distaste.

67

'Elsewhere.' Suddenly the big man turned, his shadow huge in the flame-light. 'The door will be locked – don't let that alarm you. If you hear anything – voices, movements – far off in the building, ignore it. You are safe here. No one can get in.'

There was a cold silence.

'Good night,' Brochael said calmly.

The curtain rustled. A moment later, the key grated in the lock. 'Well,' Thorkil muttered, after a moment. 'It's almost as bad as I thought. Dust, fleas, rats.' He rubbed at the soiled red cloth of his jerkin, and went off to find his own sleeping place.

Wearily, Jessa lay down in her clothes and wrapped herself in the rough, damp-smelling blankets. 'But I didn't expect Brochael,' she muttered quietly.

'What?'

There was no answer. When Thorkil came back and opened the curtain she was already asleep. He watched her for a moment, then reached out and snuffed the candle, and the flames in the eyes of the serpent on his wrist went out.

Jessa threw two crumbling squares of peat on the fire and chewed the stale bannock that seemed to be breakfast. She watched Thorkil stagger in with the empty bucket and drop it with a clang.

'That water froze as I threw it out.' He sat down, and looked at her. 'We didn't get many answers last night. No one could have got here before us, could they?'

She was thinking of the pedlar. 'I don't know. Who would?'

'And have you seen this?' He tapped the slab of goat's cheese they had found.

'Cheese,' Jessa said drily.

'Yes, but where did it come from? Where are the goats?'

That surprised her. She shook her head, thinking of the empty out-buildings and the untrodden snow. 'Perhaps in some building at the back . . .'

'They'd freeze. And Kari. Where's he?'

Jessa swallowed some crumbs. 'I don't want to know that.' She wiped her hand in her skirt. 'Locked in some room, I suppose.'

A scrape interrupted them; the key turned and Brochael ducked in under the low doorway. He had snow in his hair. He grinned at them cheerfully. 'Awake! Sleep well?'

'Yes, thank you.'

They watched him stand in front of the fire, his clothes steaming.

Thorkil glanced at Jessa. 'Look,' he said. 'Are we prisoners here? Can we go anywhere we want to?'

Brochael gave a gruff laugh. 'We're all prisoners, lad, but I'm not your keeper, if that's what you mean. But there's not much to see here. Empty rooms and snow.'

He watched them for a moment, and they waited for some word of Kari, some warning of one door not be opened, one corridor not to be explored. But all he said was, 'This was a palace once, centuries ago. They say a troll-king built it of unhewn stone, and the great road that led up here too. Perhaps the world was warmer in those days.'

He turned and began banking up the fire. Jessa couldn't wait any longer. 'What about Kari?'

'Kari's here,' he said, without turning. 'But you won't see him.'

Afterwards they put on coats and went outside. The sky was iron-grey; a stiff wind cut into them down the side of the fell. On the white slope they could see the frozen tracks of Helgi's horses, climbing up into the fringe of trees. And all around, like a white jagged crown, were the mountains.

One courtyard at the back of the building had been swept clear of snow; in the centre was a deep well, with faint steam rising from it. As they gazed down they felt warmth on their faces. Thorkil dropped a stone in. 'A hot spring. Now that's useful.'

They tugged open doors and gazed into stables and barns and byres. Everything was held in a web of ice, glistening with a faint film of soot, as if the entire hold had once had its roofs burnt. There were no animals, not even a trace of them, but in one storehouse they found a few casks of dried apples and nuts, some cheese, and two hares hanging next to a row of smoked fish. Thorkil looked up at them.

'Fish! But where's the lake? Where are the fruit trees? Under the snow? I tell you what, Jessa, they should have starved here a long time ago. That's why she sent them here. And yet somehow they're getting this food.' He put a finger inside the silver ring on his wrist and eased it round. 'Someone must be bringing it.'

Then they went into the Hold itself, down a long corridor paved with stone and frost. Icicles hung from every lintel and sill. There were stairs leading up; they led to more corridors and passages, and empty rooms where the wind blew in through the bare windows.

Passing one room, Jessa stopped. This one was very small and dark, with a narrow window opposite the door, through which the grey daylight fell like a wand on the floor.

Something about the window puzzled her. Thorkil was far ahead, rummaging in an old rotting chest, so she stepped in and crossed the floor. Then she put her hand up to the window and touched it.

Glass!

She had only seen it before in tiny pieces, polished, in jewellery; never like this in a thick slab. Brushing the frost from it, she took her glove off and felt the surface, saw the trapped bubbles of air deep inside.

'Jessa?' Thorkil called.

'I'm in here.'

She put her eye to the glass and looked through it. There was a courtyard below her, with trampled snow. A movement caught her eye; someone was walking through the clutter of buildings. Someone smaller than Brochael. As she tried to see, the shape warped and bent in the thick glass; slid into queer contortions. She stepped back, suddenly. Had that been Kari?

'What are you looking at?' Thorkil was at her elbow.

'Quick! There's someone out there!'

He looked out, blocking the light with his hands.

'Can you see him?' Jessa asked impatiently.

He shrugged. 'Maybe. For a second I thought there was something. Just a flicker.' He looked at her. 'Was it Kari?'

'I don't know. Someone small . . . it was all bent and twisted.'

They were silent. Then Thorkil said bleakly, 'I think I'd rather know than wonder like this.'

71

That evening sewing a tear in her sleeve, Jessa said quietly, 'How did you know we were coming?'

Brochael looked up from the fire, his face flushed with heat. 'My business.' He stirred the oatmeal, calmly.

'Someone came before us?' Thorkil ventured.

Brochael grinned. 'If you say so. I just knew, that's all. Ragnar sent you here because of your fathers. His idea of a pleasant exile. And to deliver his guilty little message.'

'Did you know,' Jessa said, biting the thread, 'that Gudrun wanted us to come as well?'

That startled him. 'She wanted it?'

'We overheard,' Jessa explained. She looked up at him closely. 'She not only knew we were coming, she said to the old man that it was her idea – that she'd made the Jarl send us.'

Brochael stared back. 'Did she say why?'

'Not really . . . it was hard to hear. She said she would have her hand on us . . . I don't know what that meant.'

'Don't you?' His face darkened; he looked older and grimmer. 'Did she give you anything to eat or drink?'

'Yes, but she drank it too.'

He shook his head. 'She's a sorceress, Jessa. That means nothing at all.'

She looked at Thorkil. 'And when can we see Kari?' she asked, trying to sound calm.

Brochael went back to stirring the porridge. 'When you're ready. When I think you're ready.' He gave them a strange, sidelong look. 'And if you really want to.'

72

10

It's safe to tell a secret to one,
Risky to tell it to two.
To tell it to three is thoughtless folly,
Everyone else will know.

Time at Thrasirshall passed slowly. Despite the mysterious supplies, food was short and Jessa often felt hungry. After a while she got used to it. The cold was still intense; they were so far north the snow still had not begun to melt. The weather made it difficult to get outside, but sometimes she and Thorkil scrambled up the fell and wandered into the silent woods. On one afternoon of pale sunshine they climbed a higher crag and gazed out at the desolate miles of land carved by slow glaciers. Brochael had told them there was nothing more to the north but ice, until the sky came down and touched the earth. Even the road ended here, at the world's end.

They ran all the way back to keep warm, floundering and giggling through the snow, Jessa in front, so that she struggled across the courtyard and burst into the room without warning. Then she stopped instantly, letting Thorkil thud into her back.

The opposite door was closing; soft footsteps shuffled on the other side, fading to an echo in empty spaces. One chair was pushed back; a knife and a piece of carven wood had been flung on the table.

Brochael leaned back and watched them, as if he was waiting for the questions. After a moment Jessa went to the fire, warming the sudden cold from her back. She watched Thorkil pick up the wood and run his fingers over the skilful carving.

'Is he afraid of us?' he said at last.

Brochael took the wood from him. 'In a way. Remember he's seen few folk beside me. But it's more than that. You're afraid of him.'

And they were. They knew it. They kept together most of the time, never went alone into the dim corridors. They spent time playing chess, mending their clothes, snaring hares, or at the unending task of fetching wood and kindling. Brochael watched them, as if he was biding his time. Some days he would vanish for hours at a time and come back without any explanation, and every night he locked the door with the iron key.

Once, late at night hauling water from the well, they thought they saw candlelight flickering in one window high in the tower, and the two black birds that had startled Helgi always seemed to be flapping and karking up there, wheeling against the greens and golds of the aurora that flickered here every night.

It was on one of those nights that Jessa had her dream.

She had fallen asleep in the warm huddle of blankets and she dreamed the pedlar came out of the darkness and put his hand on her shoulder. He shook her. 'Wake up. I haven't let you down. Look, I've melted the snow.'

She got up and crossed to a large glass window and looked out. She saw a green land, a blue sky. Flocks of birds wheeled and screamed overhead: gulls, skuas, swifts. In the courtyard horsemen were riding; each horse had eight legs, like the horse of the High One; each was black with fiery eyes.

She looked around, but the pedlar was gone, and only a white snake moved across the stone floor and under the raised bed.

Then she dreamed that the curtain opened and someone looked in. The figure crossed the room to her, looked down at her, and she saw it was Gudrun, her white hand stretched out. One finger touched Jessa's cheek with a stab of ice.

She woke at once and sat up, heart thudding.

The curtain billowed. In the next room the key was grating in the lock.

She leapt up, ran out of the booth and flung herself on the closing door. The latch jerked in her hands.

'Thorkil!' she screamed, feeling the door shudder; the wood cut her fingers. Then he was there, pulling with her. 'It's locked,' he gasped. 'Too late.'

And she knew he was right. She released the latch and stood there, listening. There was no sound, and yet they both knew he was there, standing just beyond the door.

'Kari?' Jessa said softly.

Nothing moved. There was a small knot-hole in the door. She could look through; she could see him. But she dared not.

Then they heard him walk away, into silence.

After a while they went and crouched by the hot embers of the fire; Thorkil stirred them up to a brief blaze.

'Tomorrow,' Jessa said firmly, 'we'll find him. We'll search every room and corner. Everywhere. Brochael needn't know, either.'

He sat down, easing the tight ring around his arm. 'If he's insane,' he said at last, 'he'd be dangerous.'

'Well at least we'd *know*. We've *got* to find out.' She glared at him. 'Are you coming?'

He ran a sooty hand through his hair, and frowned with annoyance. 'Of course I am. Someone has to keep an eye on you.'

In the morning they sat at the gaming board, waiting for Brochael to go out into the courtyard. At last, after five minutes, he had not come back. Jessa looked up. 'Ready?'

He shrugged. 'It's that or lose.'

They had decided to start right up at the highest part of the tower and work their way down – there was still one staircase that was complete from battlements to floor, although even that had holes. They climbed slowly, their lungs aching with the cold, opening every door, prying into the forgotten crannies of the Hall. Everything was the same as before: dark, frozen, echoing.

'The candlelight was from a window this high,' Jessa said at last. 'If we really saw it.'

'Not these rooms. No one's used them for years.' Thorkil sat wearily on the stairs, grinding the frost with his heel. After a while he said, 'Perhaps Kari is kept underground. If you think about it, it might be. Brochael has always been so sure we won't find him.'

She nodded, reluctantly. Nowhere had been

forbidden to them. Wherever Kari was, they were unlikely to find it by accident.

Thorkil got up. 'Come on.'

'Wait!' She turned quickly. 'Did you hear that?'

The corridor was a dim tunnel of stone. Dust moved in draughts over the floor. One drop of water dripped from a sill.

'What?' Thorkil muttered.

'A scrape . . . a screech. I don't know. Something alive.'

He glanced at her; her lips were pale, her gloved hands clenched in tight fists. 'I didn't hear anything.'

'But I did!' Then her eyes widened.

'Look!' she breathed.

Far down in the dimness, a door was appearing. It was forming itself out of nothing on the damp wall; a tall outline of dark wood, its latch shiny from use. A thin line of sunlight flickered underneath it, as if the room beyond was bright.

Very quietly, side by side, they approached the door. Jessa half expected it to fade away again, to be just a trick of the shadows, but it remained, waiting for them.

She reached out and put her hand on the latch. Something shifted inside; there was a rustle, and a step, and that peculiar low screech she had heard before. The latch was cold and hard under her fingers. She lifted it, and let the door swing wide.

At first she thought she was looking into her dream. The room was flooded with sunlight streaming in through an open window, a window leaded with tiny panes of thick, bubbly glass. On the sill the ice was melting; a raven perched there looking out, until the bang of the door startled it and it leapt into

77

the blue air with a screech. Someone was sitting near the window, hunched up in a chair, his back to them. A mirror was propped in front of him, and as Jessa glanced in it she saw herself and Thorkil framed in the dark doorway. Then the figure moved; he bent closer to the mirror, his straight silvery hair brushing the bronze. A throb of panic shuddered through her. He had no reflection, nothing! She saw only herself and the glitter of sunlight that filled the room.

Then Kari turned, and looked sidelong at them. She drew a sharp breath; heard Thorkil's stifled mutter.

His face was Gudrun's. They were identical.

11

What I won from her I have well used.

He uncurled himself quickly and stood up. They saw a thin boy no taller than themselves, his skin pale and his eyes colourless as glass. With two steps he was across the room, staring at Jessa, her hair, her coat, feeling the fur on it with a murmur of delight, touching amulets and luckstones lightly; then fingering the rich red cloth of Thorkil's jerkin as if he had never seen such colour. With a shock Jessa realized that he probably never had. She flicked a glance around the room and back. This was not the terrible creature of the stories. She felt foolish, confused.

Suddenly he stepped back. 'Come inside,' he said. 'Come and see where I've been hiding from you.'

Slowly, Jessa stepped forward; Thorkil hung back, near the open door. They were both alert, wary of this strange thin creature, his quick eagerness. Kari seemed not to notice. He caught Jessa's arm and made her sit on a bench, pouring water for her from a wooden jug; showing her chess pieces he had carved – tiny, intricate things, the king Brochael to the life, standing stoutly with folded arms. Despite herself, Jessa laughed.

At once Kari's mood seemed to change. He drew

back. She felt as if all the excitement had suddenly drained out of him; now he was uncertain, nervous.

'I'm sorry,' he murmured. 'I took you by surprise. I'm not what you expected.'

'No,' she said, her voice a whisper.

He picked a knife up from the table and fingered it.

Jessa stood up. Behind him she saw suddenly that the long room was hung with chunks of glass threaded on thin ropes; like crystal spiders they twirled and swung, speckling the walls with sun-light. And the walls were drawn all over with strange spirals and whorls, in dim colours. He turned and picked up the mirror. 'Come and see,' he said rather sadly. 'This is why I had to let you in. Everything has begun.' He held up the polished metal; Jessa saw only herself, her face blank with shock, and Thorkil behind her like a shadow. Kari looked at them.

'Can you see him?' he asked. 'The man in the mirror?'

She felt Thorkil tremble. Her own hands shook. When she spoke she hardly recognized her voice. 'Yes. We can both see him. Clearly.' She watched her own mouth mumble the lie. Then Thorkil gripped her arm and drew her back.

To their surprise the boy smiled and shook his head. 'You think I'm insane,' he said. 'I'd forgotten the rumours she puts about.' He caught Jessa's eye and his face was grave again. 'But the man is there. Look, Jessa, both of you. Look hard.'

Sunlight glimmered in the mirror, stabbing her eyes like white pain. The polished surface blurred; she saw a sudden glint, a candle flame in a dark room, ominously dark, hung with rich, heavy cloths. In the middle of the mirror, on a great bed, lay a man richly dressed, his eyes open, his hands clasped rigid on an unsheathed sword. She recognized him at once.

Then the sun glinted; the mirror was yellow and smooth.

Before Jessa could speak, footsteps came along the corridor, and Brochael blocked the doorway. His face was a study in astonishment.

'I had to,' Kari said quickly. 'All our plans will have to begin, Brochael. The snow will melt, and she'll come for us.'

'Gudrun?' Jessa stammered.

'There's nothing to stop her.' He put the mirror down and spread his thin white fingers out over it. 'He's dead, Brochael. The Jarl is dead.'

Without a word or a murmur of surprise Brochael sat down on an old chest near the door. Then he thumped the door frame. 'She's finished him! I knew she would!'

Jessa went cold.

'How was he when you saw him?' Brochael asked.

She thought back to the Jarl sitting in his carven chair, his hard stare into the flames of the fire. 'The last time,' she remembered, 'he was shrunken. Dried up. But he was well, still strong. There was nothing wrong with him.'

'Exactly. Nor with the Jarl before him – until she killed him.' Brochael reached up and caught her arm. 'Sit down, girl. You look bewildered.'

She sat herself down next to him; his great arm crept round her shoulders. 'I can understand it,' he said. 'And it's the shock too of seeing such a monster and creature of horrors as this, I suppose.'

He gave Kari a wide grin.

The boy smiled back, then got up and wandered over to the window. He was very thin; his clothes, like Brochael's, were a cobweb of patches, sewn here and there with large, irregular stitches. He sat on the windowsill and leaned out.

'I watched you from up here, many times.'

'We didn't see you,' Thorkil said.

'No.' Kari turned to look at him, Gudrun's look of secret, close knowledge. 'And neither did you see the door to this room, though you passed it more than once.'

Thorkil frowned, fingering the arm-ring.

Brochael's arm was warm and comfortable; Jessa leaned back against it. A sudden wave of relief washed over her. A shadow had lifted. Only now could she realize how she had dreaded to meet Kari – how she had not let herself imagine what he might be.

'So it was you who knew we were coming,' she said, thinking aloud.

With a kark and a flap one of the ravens flew in through the window on to the sill. Kari held out a finger, and the bird tugged at it gently. 'I watched you come. I saw you in the storm, and then, again, at the village called Trond. There is some power there, that old woman sits in a web of it. She often thinks about me.' He stroked the bird's stiff feathers. 'I've watched her thoughts.'

'Is it the mirror?' Thorkil asked curiously, picking it up and turning it over. 'Can you see things in that, anything you want to?'

Kari seemed lost in thought; it was Brochael who answered. 'Not just the mirror. Anything will do – ice, water, the side of a cup. He has her powers, Thorkil. That's what she's afraid of, the reason she brews all those filthy rumours.' He glanced at Kari and lowered his voice. 'The reason she locked her son away and never even let him be seen.'

Jessa felt him quiver, as if anger seethed in him. Kari turned. 'You shouldn't speak of it if it upsets you.'

Brochael stood up suddenly and crossed to the fire. He began to fling kindling on to it, hard and fast, as if he hardly saw what he was doing. Watching him, Kari said, 'She kept me in a room, at the Jarls-hold. I saw no one but her, and the old dwarf, Grettir. Sometimes I think I remember a woman, a different face, but only briefly. There was only dark-ness and silence in that place, long years of it; of shadows and sunlight moving slowly down the walls. Ice and sun and ice again, and voices and pictures moving in my head. She would come and speak bitter, fierce things, or she would just watch me stumbling away from her.

'Then Brochael came. I don't remember the jour-ney, or the snow – isn't that strange? Just this room instead of that one, and this great shambling man who came and talked and put his arm round me.' He half smiled at them. 'No one had done that before. It felt strange, and yet I liked it. He taught me to speak, and to run, and to go outside without feeling terror of such open places. When she came and tor-mented my dreams he woke me. Thrasirshall was no prison for me, Jessa. It was my freedom.'

He paused, and looked down at the mirror. 'Now we have to leave it.'

'Are you certain he's dead?' Thorkil put in abruptly.

'Yes.'

'She may not have done it,' Jessa muttered.

Brochael shook his head. 'Oh, it has her mark. She has chosen her time; she's ready. And you read his message – that was from a man expecting something. Now she'll send her swordsmen out here. They may already be on the way. We have two, maybe three, days.' He looked at Kari. 'Was the death today?'

Kari nodded. They were silent a moment.

'Where can we go?' Jessa thought of the ice-covered fells and moors.

'Oh, I've still got a few friends.' Brochael gazed artlessly out of the window. 'We're not entirely alone.'

'The ones who bring your food,' Thorkil muttered.

The big man turned and grinned at him. 'I knew you were puzzled by that. It's been goading you like a gnat, hasn't it?'

'Who are they?'

'Wait and see.'

Jessa was chewing the ends of her hair. She thought how sudden everything was. 'But there's nowhere we can go where she can't see us.'

'Or where I can't see her.' Kari sat on the chair by the window, his knees huddled up. 'She'll hunt us, yes, like a wolf, sly and sudden, but I'll know. She and I are the same.' He glanced up at Brochael, a bleak, swift look. 'And we have no choice, do we?'

'None at all,' Brochael murmured.

12

Brand kindles brand till they burn out,
Flame is quickened by flame.

They spent the rest of the day preparing for a hard
journey. All the supplies of food were brought in
from the outhouses; two hares that Brochael found
in his snares were cooked and cut up. Water would
not be a problem. The snow still lay here on the
high ground, and as they travelled down, Brochael
said, they would find the rivers awash with meltwater. Still, Jessa took care to bring in a few buckets
from the hot spring and wash in luxury. She knew
it would be a long time before that would happen
again.

Kari moved about downstairs, watching Brochael
for a while, then he wandered outside, the birds
flapping and hopping after him. Thorkil followed;
Jessa closed the door behind them. Sitting down at
the table next to Brochael, feeling clean and warm,
she said, 'You misled us, didn't you? Deliberately.'

'Not me. They're Gudrun's stories. You should
blame her.'

After a moment Jessa said, 'It's hard to believe she
could spin such lies, even her. . . . Kari is so . . .'

'Ordinary?' Brochael asked slyly.

'Well no. Of course not . . .'

Brochael laughed. 'Exactly. He's her image, Jessa, her copy. They say when he was born the midwife screamed out in horror – she could see, I suppose, that this was another of the Snow-walkers, another sorcerer. And Gudrun, I often wonder what she must have thought about this rival, the only one who might ever threaten her. So she shut him away and let the rumours run.'

Jessa looked up. 'And why didn't she kill him? Many babies die. It wouldn't have seemed so strange.'

Brochael stopped his work. For a moment he did not answer; then he said, 'That's what worries me, Jessa. It's worried me for years. She wants him for something. And I don't want to think about what.'

Later, as she picked out her warmest clothes and squashed them into a pack, she heard Thorkil come in behind her. He closed the door of the room softly.

'Brochael says take as little as you can,' she said. 'We'll have to carry everything ourselves, remember.'

He muttered something, and sat down. She turned her head.

'What's wrong?'

Thorkil laughed briefly. 'Nothing! We're leaving this place, for a start. That makes me happy enough.'

'Does it?' She threaded the laces of the bag swiftly. 'I didn't want to come here either – I think I was more frightened than you, even – but since I've been here I've been happy, in an odd sort of way. And now we know Kari's not . . .'

'Yes!' Thorkil breathed a sigh of exasperation. 'Kari! Thinking he was some sort of deformed creature was bad, but I'm not sure the truth isn't worse. He's *her*, Jessa. Everytime he looks at me I shiver.'

'No,' she said, shaking her head. 'He's not her. He just looks the same. But that doesn't mean they *are* the same.'

For a moment they both sat side by side, thinking.

Then she pulled his hair playfully. 'Worrier. Be a warrior. And I see you're still wearing the lady's present, anyway.'

He shrugged, and touched the arm-ring. 'That's because it won't come off.'

Surprised, Jessa looked at it. 'I thought it was loose enough before?'

'A bit looser. Perhaps the cold here has made it shrink. Anyway, it won't come off, and it doesn't matter. No one can steal it, this way.'

She put her hand on the smooth snake and tugged at it, but he was right. It gripped his wrist without a gap.

'Perhaps it's swallowed a bit more of its tail,' he laughed.

There was something in his voice for a moment that was new to her: a strange tone, but when she looked at him he laughed and stood up, his longish brown hair brushing the collar of the red jerkin. 'Don't worry, Jessa, I won't bring much. I may like fine things, but I'm too lazy to carry them far!'

And they both laughed, in the cold room.

That evening, around the fire in the darkness downstairs, they made their plans.

'We'll go south,' Brochael said. 'After all, it's the only way you can go from this godforsaken place. To the north is nothing but ice, mountains and seas of it, and mists. Beyond that, Gunningagap, the rift into blackness. Only sorcerers could live up there.'

Jessa flicked a glance at Kari; he sat curled up against Brochael's knees, his face a shifting mask of firelight and shadows.

'And then where?' Thorkil asked. 'A ship?'

'No ship would take us,' Brochael said curtly. 'And I don't intend to try. The weather's beginning to turn milder. Spring is coming. We'll go overland – it will be hard, but safer. And there's a place – an old hall, one of the Wulfings' hunting halls in the mountains. That's the place we're going.'

'Will we be safe there?' Jessa asked, surprised.

Brochael shrugged. 'As anywhere. But that's the meeting place. It's all been arranged, long ago. The Jarl's death will bring them.'

Kari shifted, as if the fire scorched him. One of the ravens gave a low croak; the flames crackled and hissed over damp wood.

'And after?' Thorkil insisted. 'What then? Will these mysterious allies of yours have swordsmen, horses, axemen? Will they fight against Gudrun?'

'We'll see.' Brochael gave his rich laugh. 'You're very curious, aren't you, lad.'

Thorkil shrugged. 'Wary, that's all.'

And then Kari said, very quietly, 'We should start tomorrow.'

Brochael looked at him.

After a moment he said, 'What is it?'

'A ship.' Kari watched the flames; his voice was quiet. 'A ship with a dragon prow. She's beached, on a rocky shore.'

'Can you show us?' Brochael kept his voice low.

Kari did not answer. His gaze seemed to be on

something deep in the fire; Jessa stared too, trying to see.

And then, in the shifting of a burnt log, the ship was there. She saw it through the flames, as if it was behind them, a little beyond. Horses were being led off, down a steep ramp into the water that swirled and sank through the shingle. Men stood about, some holding torches that guttered and spat. She could smell pitch and resin, the salt tang of the fjord, hear a gull crying, far off.

'That's Trond.' Thorkil's voice came out of the darkness. Jessa nodded. She had already recognized the steep cliffs, and among a group of men, Sigmund Greycloak, his hair swept across his face by the night wind.

But the men coming from the boat were some she had seen about the Jarlshold; silent, rough men, each with a serpent mark tattooed down his cheek – Gudrun's own choice. She counted ten or more. An ashen shield was flung down, then spears, heavy packs. Then the flames flickered in the draught, and there was only darkness behind the fire.

She looked at Brochael. 'How can they have got so far already? It's impossible. It took us three days to reach Trond . . .'

His bleak expression answered her; she caught her breath as the thought leapt into her mind. 'She sent them out *before*? Before Ragnar was dead?'

Brochael nodded silently, rubbing his beard. For a while no one spoke, each of them thinking. Jessa felt again that sudden surge of panic that she had known so long ago in the Jarl's Hall; could almost think she smelt Gudrun's sweet scent, hear the drift and rustle of her movements.

Raising her head, she stared at the flames.

Gudrun looked back at her.

The sorceress was surrounded by candles; a halo of light that lit the sharpness of her smile, the eager glint of her eyes.

Transfixed with fear, Jessa hardly breathed, but Kari stretched out his foot and nudged a log. It shifted, with a shower of sparks. Wood fell, settled. The fire leapt up; it showed Jessa the dark room, Kari's face with a bleak pain in it, Brochael's grim and angry.

'Did she see us?' Thorkil whispered.

'No.' Kari's fingers shook; he clenched them. 'She tries – often. But I won't let her. Not any more.'

Behind him, something shuffled in the darkness. The raven, with a hop and a flutter, perched on the chair behind Brochael's shoulder. It's eyes were tiny red sparks in the flamelight.

13

Odin, they said, swore an oath on his ring;
Who from now on will trust him?

They left at mid-morning. Brochael had food ready.
They ate it quickly, in a tense silence. Jessa watched
Kari until he glanced at her with his sharp look, then
she smiled. Doubtfully, he smiled back.

When everything was ready Brochael flung water
on the fire and hauled a heavy pack on to his back.
He picked up an axe and shoved it into his belt.
'Well, I brought little; I'm taking away less.' He
grinned at Jessa. 'It will be interesting to see how
the world has changed.'

Outside, they wrapped themselves in cloaks and
hoods and thick gloves. The wind was cold; it was
coming from the north and brought flecks of snow.
Overhead the two ravens flapped against the clouds.

'They'll miss you,' Jessa said.

Kari looked up. 'They're coming. They go where
I go.'

He turned and looked back at the Hall, at the
black walls trapped in their gleaming coats of ice.
'It's strange,' he whispered. 'I feel as if I'm stepping
out of myself, like a snake out of its skin.'

'Come on.' Brochael caught his arm. 'If her men
catch us here, that's just what we'll all be doing.'

Kari pulled a dark, ragged scarf up around his face. Then Brochael led them across the courtyard and under the broken archway, out into the snow.

All that long afternoon they walked, one in the footsteps of the other, up the long slopes of the mountain. The wind whistled against them, as if it would push them back; the snow underfoot was soft under the top layer of thin, crunchy ice. They crossed the glacier carefully, slithering on the flat snow swirls, watching for cracks and crevasses, moving swiftly on the scree and tumbled stones. Once over, they climbed again, along the sheer side of the fell, heading south, floundering through the soft, wetter snow. By the time they reached the top the sky was dark purple, with a few stars scattered across it, faint as dust. Far off in the north, a pale aurora flickered over the mountain peaks.

Jessa was wet through and breathless. She paused, looking back at the long blue scar they had torn through the snow.

Brochael looked too. 'It's a dry night,' he muttered. 'That will still be there tomorrow – maybe even the day after. They'll see it.'

She looked at him. 'They'll be here tomorrow?'

'Bound to be. They'll ride hard.' He turned and trudged on after Kari and Thorkil. 'When Gudrun wants a thing done, Jessa, it's done.'

By about midnight they had come back down to the treeline. Brochael let them sleep for a while in a thick pinewood, where the trees clustered so closely there was no snow; they lay on a centuries-thick quilt of needles and leaf-mould, richly scented and full of tiny, scurrying beetles. Too tired to notice, Jessa slept.

The ravens woke her; croaking in the trees above her, sending down showers of dry powdery snow. She sat up. Brochael and Kari were out at the trees' edge, talking. She saw Brochael mark something on the ground with a stick. Thorkil lay nearby, still asleep, his fur hood up over his face, one arm thrown out carelessly. She shivered; it was barely light and bitterly cold. Brochael turned.

'About time. Come and have something to eat.'

It was the same cooked meat, and some black, hard bread. She chewed it slowly, looking out over the still, white country wrapped in its fogs and mists; the forests marching over slope and hillside like a motionless and silent army. Kari stared out too, as if his eyes feasted on this different place. She caught the same vivid excitement in him as when he had first seen Thorkil and herself; his fingers clenched in their gloves, his eyes paler than ever in the early light. Finally Brochael stirred and flung a handful of rotten cones at Thorkil.

'Get up, lad. This is no place to sleep late.' He turned to Jessa. 'Get your things. Time's wasting.'

It took them a while to wake Thorkil; he seemed deep in dreams and hardly knew where he was for a moment or two. Brochael grinned down at him.

'Perhaps the young lord could get off his bed now? And take his scented bath?'

Thorkil smiled back, but Jessa thought he was still quiet and tired.

Once they had begun to walk none of them spoke

93

very much; it was easier to trudge in silence through the empty land and the wide, bitter sky.

Suddenly, at about midday, Kari stopped. Then, slowly, he looked back. Jessa looked too.

Smoke was rising over the skyline, far off – a great black column of it, the underside lit with a faint red glow. Silent, the four of them watched it. It could only be Thrasirshall. They'd been quick, Jessa thought, quicker than she'd dreamed. Gudrun must have chosen them well; men who wouldn't fear the place and its hidden creature – perhaps she'd even told them something of the truth. They'd have searched, then burnt, and even now they would be galloping down the fellside. She turned, straight into Brochael. His face was grim. 'Yes, you're right. Kari! Come on!'

He pushed them into the trees and along the hill-top. The snow was thinner here, and in the tangle of undergrowth their tracks would be harder to see. Jessa knew he was worried; he urged them on tire-lessly all afternoon. Kari walked swiftly, and she wasn't tired herself. Oddly enough it was Thorkil who held them back. More than once she had to call the others to wait for him.

When he caught up, his breath came in gasps and he clutched his side.

'Can't we rest?' he said at last.

'What's the matter with you?' Brochael snarled. 'Are you ill?'

'I don't know!' He seemed puzzled, and in pain. 'I can't seem to get my breath . . . perhaps it's the cold. Just a few minutes, Brochael.'

But Brochael shoved him on. 'We haven't got that

long. A spear in the back will be a harder pain to put up with.'

But after a while Thorkil stopped again. He collapsed on to his knees, dragging in air. Jessa crouched beside him.

'He's really in trouble. We'll have to wait.'

Brochael stormed and cursed. Then he turned and marched off through the trees.

'Where's he gone?' Jessa asked.

'To look back.' Kari knelt beside her. He took his thin hand from its glove and gripped Thorkil's shoulder.

'Look at me,' he said.

Shuddering, Thorkil looked up. Their eyes met. They were still for a moment, a long silence, and then Thorkil began to breathe easily and freely. At the same time Kari shivered, as if something had chilled him. He put his glove back on and pushed the lank hair from his eyes.

'What was it?' Jessa said to him.

'Nothing.' His pale eyes searched through the trees. 'Nothing. He'll be all right.'

With a floundering of branches Brochael was coming back. 'No sign of them yet,' he snapped. The forest ends ahead, then the land is open moor. We'll have to cross it before tonight.' He looked at Thorkil. 'Can you manage?'

'Yes.' Jessa helped him up; he straightened slowly. 'It's easier now. . . . I don't know what caused it.'

'Never mind! Just move.'

They pushed their way out through the trees, the wet, heavy snow sliding from the branches on to their shoulders. Beyond, the land was a dim slope, frozen into stiff hillocks and littered with boulders under the snow. It was treacherous, but they scrambled down. Far overhead the two birds circled; they swooped down, cawing and karking over Kari's head as he slipped and stumbled at Jessa's side. Below, Brochael was close to Thorkil, both of them sliding on the loose scree that lay invisible under the snow. Horses would find this hard to manage. That would help surely.

By the time they had crossed the great moor the short day was darkening. They were tired; their ankles ached with the bruising of the stones. Before them lay a small lake, frozen white, but at its edge the land made an overhang where rock outcropped. The bitter wind brought tears to their eyes. Jessa's ears ached and her toes were an agony.

Brochael pushed his way through the scrub and under the overhang and they followed, squatting in a breathless row against the rock.

In the shelter and the quiet they coughed and spat and caught breath. Jessa felt Brochael's warmth glow at her side. She tugged her boots off and rubbed her wet feet. After a while a faint glow touched her face and fingers.

'Well,' Brochael said at last. 'Here is as good as anywhere.'

'You mean we'll stay?' Thorkil said doubtfully.

'We can't outrun them. We must hide.' He looked at Kari. 'Will the birds warn us?'

The boy nodded, tugging pine needles from his silvery hair.

'Then we sleep,' Brochael said. 'All of us. While we can.'

'It's too cold,' Thorkil objected. 'We'll freeze – or we will later.'

Brochael gave him an irritated glance. 'I don't think you'll find that, if you're as tired as you should be. You were the one who wanted to stop.'

'Yes.' Thorkil looked uneasy. 'Yes I know.'

They ate some dried meat from Brochael's pack, but it was hard to swallow and there was nothing to drink but snow. Then they lay down, huddled together for warmth. Jessa felt Brochael pull his coat around Kari. Then she slept, suddenly and completely.

When she woke it was still dark, the sky in the east glimmering with wan light. She was unbearably stiff and cold. Carefully she moved away from the others and sat up. Brochael lay on his back against the rocks, one hand on his axe even in sleep. She could just see Kari in the depths of his coat. But Thorkil was gone.

She scrambled up, easing the pain from her back and arms. Then, quietly, so as not to wake the others, she pushed through the bushes and crouched down.

The landscape was bleak, and silent. Far off some bird was calling, a lonely cry over the miles of tundra. The wind was cold, but she knew it was milder than last night; already the frost on the branches under her fingers was beginning to drip.

But where was Thorkil? She was worried about him. The pain yesterday, which seemed to fade so quickly – that wasn't like him.

She slipped out from the bushes and stood up. Below, over a shallow slope of scree, was the shore of the lake, its black reeds poking up from the frozen lid. Perhaps he was down there.

She went down, the tiny stones trickling

97

underfoot, and saw at the very edge that the ice was receding, thinning to a frill where bubbles of trapped air slid and wheezed. She crouched down and drank; the water was bitterly cold and stagnant.

Then a sound froze her. It was the slow clip-clop of hooves. It came from her left, somewhere nearby. As she looked round, she saw him, a horseman coming down the track, an armed man, with ring mail that glittered in the pale light. She kept perfectly still. If she moved now he would see her.

The man drew rein. He looked across the dimness of the moor, at the flat glimmer of the ice. Where were the rest of them? she wondered. Probably not far.

His head turned; she held her breath, flattening against the wet stones, but he kept looking, beyond her. Then he urged the horse on.

At the same moment she saw Thorkil.

He was crouched behind a rock halfway up the slope. He hadn't seen her, but he was watching the rider, intently, and then he did something that astonished her. He stood up, and called!

The rider's head turned swiftly; the horse whinnied with fright. As the horseman struggled with it, Jessa leapt to her feet, and Thorkil looked down at her. He stared, as if she was a stranger. At the same time the horseman dragged the horse's head to stillness. He looked up, and she saw him stiffen.

He had seen her!

14

If aware that another is wicked, say so:
Make no truce or treaty with foes.

The horseman stared at Jessa. After a moment he urged the horse with his knees, and it picked its way towards her over the stones. The man's eyes slid from her; he paused as if puzzled, and then came on again.

'Keep very still,' Kari's voice said, from somewhere behind her. 'He can't see you now, but if you move it will be more difficult.'

She waited, as the horseman rode nearer. Now she could see his face, the blue snakemark in his skin; he looked wary, almost afraid. His eyes took in the moor and the lake; they moved across her without a flicker. It was uncanny, unbearably tense. She moved her foot; a stone clicked.

Again the man stopped, his gaze exploring the lakeshore. She was so close she could have reached out and touched the horse. It turned and looked at her, nuzzling at her shoulder.

Suddenly, as if his nerve had snapped, the rider whirled his mount around and urged it hurriedly back up the track, slithering and scrambling over the loose ground. He rode up to the top of the slope and over it, without looking back. The noise of hooves on stones died away to silence.

A warm hand gripped her. 'It's all right. He's gone.'

Brochael was there, holding his axe, looking at her angrily. 'Why did you stand up? If he'd seen any one of us, one shout would have brought them all over here. Are you mad?'

'I thought he would see Thorkil!'

'Thorkil was well hidden,' Brochael snorted, watching him come down the slope. 'Think, next time!'

Furious, she pulled away from him. She glared at Thorkil angrily. 'Why did *you* stand up?' she snapped.

He glared back. 'I was calling you. I hadn't seen the rider.'

'But . . .'

'Anyway, it doesn't matter,' he said. 'I climbed up there to get a look around. You can see the line of the old road across the hills. It looks as if it heads south.'

While he and Brochael discussed the route, she turned away, puzzled. She saw Kari watching her. He sat on a rock, with one of the great birds at his feet, the other behind him, picking at something red on the snow. For a moment he looked so like Gudrun that she shivered.

'How did you do it?' she asked.

'I don't know.' His eyes met hers, calmly. 'It wasn't easy – for a moment he saw you. I had to make him believe that he was wrong. That there was nothing there.'

'Like the door, in the Hall?'

'Yes.'

She turned and looked out at the coming sun lighting the clouds and the white mountains. 'Is it the runes, the magic the old woman has? Is that the same?'

He shrugged. 'I don't know any runes. This is in me, I haven't learned it.' He looked over at the lake. 'I've never seen so much frozen water, like that. It has a strange beauty . . .'

'Has it?' Jesse asked. 'It tastes foul.'

They ate some meat and smoked fish, and drank the brackish water. Then Brochael outlined his plans.

'We'll head directly south, keeping near the line of the road, but staying in the forests as far as possible. We'll be harder to follow there; we might even risk a fire at night.'

'What if they have dogs?' Jessa asked.

'They don't. We would have seen them by now. It will be rough country, but if we move quickly we could be at Morthrafell in two days, where the river called Skolka cuts through the mountains down to Skolkafjord and the sea.' He glanced at Kari. 'We can wait at the hall of the Wulfings, as arranged.'

'Wait for who?' Thorkil asked.

Ignoring him, Brochael pulled the pack on to his back and stood up. 'Now take care. They may still be about.'

It took them all morning to cross the open moor, going cautiously over the boggy, treacherous ground. Finally the land rose a little, and they came into the forest, scattering a herd of elk.

Here the snow was thin; ice glistened and hung

from the dark branches. They moved easily through the scattered trees, and as the sun climbed it became warmer. A few birds sang, far down in the aisles of the wood.

Jessa tried to speak to Thorkil but he was never near her. He kept near Kari, always talking and asking questions which Kari rarely answered. But when they stopped to eat at midday, Jessa saw her chance. Pulling Thorkil away she shoved him hard against a tree trunk.

'What were you thinking of?' she snapped.

'What do you mean?'

'You know! You called out!'

'To you.'

'But you didn't see me until after!'

He looked at her. His eyes were blue and clear; there was a hard look in them that was new. 'You're wrong, Jessa. I called you. Who else would I have called?'

She was silenced. She wanted to say 'the horseman' but it would be wrong, it would be foolish. But that was what was in her mind.

He pushed past her and went back to the others. She stared after him. It was unthinkable that he should betray them. Why should he? He hated Gudrun.

All afternoon the forest went on endlessly, full of the piping of invisible birds. They travelled along tracks and winding paths, always keeping the sun on their right as it sank among clouds and vapour. Once Kari cried out; Brochael raced back. 'What is it?'

The boy stood stock-still, his face white. 'She spoke to me. She knows where we are. She has a hand on us, gripping us tight.' He looked up at

Brochael; Jessa saw a strange glance pass between them.

After that they moved more carefully. Twice the ravens karked a warning and they plunged off the path, hiding in scrub and spiny bushes, but no one passed. Once, far off in the forest Jessa thought she heard voices and the jingle of harness, but it was so distant she could not be sure.

At sunset they were still travelling, over the high, bare passes of the hills. Jessa was desperately tired; she stumbled and her ears ached with the cold. She longed for shelter and hot food.

But now Brochael would not stop. He hurried them on over one ridge and another, perilously outlined against the black horizon. They spent part of the night in a cave high up on a cliffside; a chilly crack in the rocks, so cold that they had to risk a fire of wet wood that smoked so much they could hardly breathe. Brochael was anxious; Thorkil silent and morose. Each of them had a weapon to hand, except Kari, who slept silently and completely on the hard floor with the two birds sitting hunched by his side.

They left the cave long before it was light and climbed up, over the highest crags and passes, until at last they stood looking down on a distant green country cracked open by a great fjord of blue water.

'Skolkafjord,' Brochael said, easing the weight on his back. 'We've done well.'

The wind roared in their ears, whipping Jessa's hair out of her hood. She watched Kari, as he stared with delight at the snowless country, at the expanse of water and the distant glimmering sea. Brochael watched him too, grinning, but Thorkil stood slightly apart, looking back.

Coming down was easier. Soon they came to country Brochael recognized; thin woodlands where the snow was softer, and where small, swift streams bubbled and leapt downhill. By mid-afternoon they reached the place he had called the hall of the Wulfings.

It rose among the trees ahead of them as they came down the valley of a swift stream; a ruin without a roof and with the walls broken and blackened. Charred timbers rose from tangles of brier and bramble, and openings that had once been doors and windows were choked with black, tangled stems. Thorkil touched a window shutter that hung from one hinge; it slithered and fell with a crash that sent echoes through the wood.

Forcing his way through, Brochael led them in.

Even now they could see where the great hall had been; the large square hearth in the centre was still black with ashes, its stones fire-marked under the pine sapling that grew out of it. Jessa threw down her pack and sat on a stone; from the charred ash she pulled a half-burnt wooden spoon, its handle carved with a zigzag line.

'What happened here?'

'This was Wulfings' land,' Brochael said. 'The Jarl's men would have cleared it, and then burned it.'

With a squalk and a flap a raven landed on the high crumbling wall. Thorkil looked up at it. 'Is it safe?'

Brochael handed out broken bannocks. 'Safe as

anywhere – it's probably been long forgotten.' Jessa noticed his glance at Kari; the boy nodded slightly.

'That witch can probably see us anyway,' he went on cheerfully, stretching out his legs.

They found a sheltered place under the wall and made it as comfortable as they could, tugging out the brambles and flattening the ground, but there could be no fire until after dark, and even then it might not be wise. Jessa and Kari scrambled down to the stream for water. As he bent over it she saw him pause, and then squat, slowly. He watched the moving water with a strange fixity, always one spot, though Jessa could see nothing but the brown stream over its stones.

After a moment she asked, 'What do you see?'

Slowly, he put his hand out and spread it flat on the surface, letting the icy stream well around his fingers. Then he pulled them out and let them drip. 'Nothing.'

Absently he filled the bowl, and she knew he was going to ask her something. She was right.

'You met her, didn't you, in the Jarlshold?'

'Yes.' She had already noticed that he never called Gudrun his mother.

'You told Brochael she knew you were coming.'

'Yes.'

He looked at her intently, a sudden swift glance. Then he said, 'We're carrying something with us, Jessa, something extra. Some burden. You know that, don't you?'

She wanted to tell him about Thorkil, but she couldn't.

In silence he stood up, holding the bowl steady,

105

not to spill a drop. They walked back without speaking.

That night they risked a fire and sat around it. The heat was a glorious comfort; Jessa felt it warming her chapped hands and sore face. But she was tired of smoked meat and dry, hard oatcake, and longed for something fresh and sweet. Apples from Horolfstead, or one of Marrika's sweet honey-cakes.

As she rolled in her blanket she noticed Thorkil moving up next to Kari. There was something anxious pushing at the back of her mind, something important that she could not quite grasp, and as she reached for it it slid away, into a deep dark hole under the earth. Her mind slid after it, into sleep.

A birdscreech woke her.

She sat up in the darkness. Something moved beside her; she saw the flash of a knife and she yelled. Quick as an eel, Kari rolled over, but the knife slashed him across shoulder and chest. Then Thorkil was on him, struggling, holding him down. Jessa was already on her feet, but before she or Brochael could move, Thorkil was flung backwards with a force that astonished them. He screamed, dropping the knife and shuddering in apparent agony on the charred ground. 'Stop it!' he screamed. 'Stop him! Stop him!'

Kari scrambled up and looked down at him, his eyes cold and amused, like Gudrun's.

A coiled adder, the ice of a night . . .
A witch's welcome, the wit of a slave,
Are never safe: let no man trust them . . .

'Let him be,' Brochael said.

Kari glanced at him and seemed to do nothing else, but with a gasp Thorkil was released. He lay sprawling in the brambles, sobbing. Jessa moved towards him but Brochael caught her by the arm.

'Not yet,' he said gruffly.

Carefully, Kari went forward, blood seeping through his shirt. He crouched down and touched Thorkil's hair, very softly. Thorkil did not move. Gently, Kari's fingers moved over the heaving shoulder, down the arm to Thorkil's wrist; then he tugged the sleeve back and touched the ring. 'This is it.'

Brochael edged forward. 'An arm-ring?'

'It looks like one.'

He fingered it curiously; in the darkness Jessa saw the silver glitter. Then she clutched Brochael's sleeve.

Under Kari's touch the metal had begun to move. It softened into a long, lithe form, writhing around Thorkil's wrist, unwinding and gliding with a tiny hissing sound that chilled them. Thorkil squirmed, but Kari held him down. 'Keep still!'

Slowly, the long white worm slithered out, leaving a bloodless ring on the skin. It lay on the charred soil, twisting and kinking itself, hissing and spitting, its tiny eyes like pale beads. As they watched, it faded to dull smoke, then to a stinking smear on the soil, then to nothing.

Silently, Jessa touched all her amulets in turn. Brochael scuffed at the ground with his boot, but nothing was there. Whatever it had been, it was gone. After a moment he let her go, and she went over to Thorkil and helped him to sit up. He seemed half dazed, scratching at the white scar on his wrist as if it itched or ached unbearably. When she spoke to him he did not answer.

After a while Brochael had to come over and carry him back to the blankets, where he sank instantly into sleep.

'It wasn't him . . .' Jessa said.

'I know.' Brochael looked down at him. 'It was her.'

He crossed to Kari and began to examine the knife-slash – it was long but shallow, in places barely breaking the skin.

'We knew she had her hand on him,' Kari said.

Jessa was silent. She sat down, and handed Brochael the bowl of clean water. 'You didn't trust us. That's why we didn't see you at Thrasirshall.'

'Not until you had to.' Kari watched, as Brochael wiped the thin line of blood away.

'It's not deep,' Jessa said.

'No,' Brochael snapped, 'but it could have been. It could have been deep enough to end all her worries.'

She was silent. She knew he was right.

'And you!' the big man growled fiercely, 'you knew about this ring, but you said nothing!'

She felt the heat rise in her neck and face. 'I thought it was just his greed, I didn't think it was harmful . . .'

But it wasn't true. She was furious with herself because she had doubted Thorkil and she had been right.

Kari was watching her closely. 'There were two. You threw yours into the sea,' he said suddenly.

She shrugged, not bothering to ask how he knew. She felt ashamed and bitter.

'The ring explains a lot,' Kari said after a while. 'That pain he had – it was real enough, but she made him feel it. She's done that to me . . . long ago. It was to slow us down. And then it explains the red cloth.'

'What cloth?'

Kari put his hand into the pack at his side and pulled out a few frayed strips of cloth; a rich, red fabric with skeins of gold woven through it.

'Recognize it?'

'It's Thorkil's tunic.'

'He's been dropping bits of it,' Brochael muttered, flinging the bloody water from the bowl into the bushes. 'Stabbing pieces on to thorns, snapping branches. He was leaving a clear trail for them.'

She was aghast. 'But he hates her!'

'Even so. She moved his will; she can do that. He'll hate her even more after this.'

'Brochael found these at first by accident. Then I told the birds to pick them up.' Kari eased his arm back into his shirt. 'They like bright things. They brought them to me.'

Jessa looked out into the black forest. So this was why he had stood up that morning by the lake – so that the horseman would see him and know. She frowned, thinking of it. All this time the witch had held him by the wrist, moved him like a piece in a game.

'Do you think he knows,' she said. 'Does he understand what he's been doing?'

But Kari was staring across the ruined hall. 'Brochael . . .'

'I know. I heard it.' The big man already had the axe in his hands; it glinted in the dark.

Jessa strained her ears to catch any sound, but the forest outside the wall seemed utterly still, the breeze barely moving the branches.

Then a twig cracked.

Brochael's fingers closed slowly on the wooden shaft.

Someone was coming, rustling through the leaves. She could hear it now even over the thudding of her heart, the pliant branches of alder and blackthorn whipping back into place.

Brochael crouched lower. 'Keep still,' he breathed, 'and do nothing.' She saw movement in the broken doorway of the hall; a deeper shadow in the shadows. It paused in the tangle of branch and stone. Then, to her astonishment, it spoke.

'You can put that axe away, Brochael.'

The voice was familiar, a sly, amused tone. Brochael gave a great guffaw of laughter, and even Kari smiled.

'You rogue,' the big man roared, standing up. 'Come in here and let us see you.'

A thin shape detached itself from the shadows and pushed through the bushes. Brochael tossed down the axe and gripped him by both shoulders.

'Not so hard,' the man laughed.

'You won't snap. You're early we hadn't expected you yet.'

Jessa looked at Kari in astonishment. 'It's the pedlar!'

'What pedlar?'

The pedlar grinned at her. 'That's how she saw me last, spell-master. I was flinging a few herbs in the Jarl's fire. A certain outlaw escaped at the time.'

'And then at Wormshold,' Jessa muttered.

'Indeed. Where you were so unwilling to take the sea path, the whales' way, the house of the skerries. Frightened of what was waiting in the grim hall.' He winked at Kari. 'She was so urgent I almost told her.'

'You're a poet,' Jessa said, with sudden understanding. She knew now why he had not wanted her to escape.

Brochael laughed. 'Of course he is. You've heard of Skapti Arnsson? He was the Wulfings' skald. Talks in riddles and cryptic lines.' He pounded the man on the shoulder. 'A pedlar of words!'

The skald glanced down at Thorkil, who was laying still against the wall. 'What happened to that one?'

'She had hold of him,' Brochael said tersely. 'A sorcery, in the shape of a silver ring.'

The skald whistled. Then he said, 'We heard Ragnar was dead two days ago. We've travelled west

111

since then, mostly by night. The forests are full of the troll-wife's men.'

'Is Wulfgar with you?' Kari asked.

'Not far off.'

'Then why doesn't he come?'

The skald grinned. 'He's waiting for the signal. And he's wary of you, ravenmaster. I told him you were no monster, but the story sticks. Shall I call him?'

Kari nodded, pulling his coat about him. He looked paler in the darkness; the thin moon rising over the branches glinted on his hair. The skald went out into the wood. They heard a swish of branches, the low murmur of voices. Then he came back, followed by the man Jessa had seen in the Jarlshold, the lithe, dark-haired man in the leather coat. He came forward quickly, his eyes glancing over Brochael and herself until he came to Kari, and he stopped. They stood staring at each other, one pale and one dark.

Wulfgar spoke first. 'She's an accomplished liar,' he said, almost admiringly. 'You have all her looks.'

Kari looked down absently and then gazed at Wulfgar. 'Not her heart,' he said.

Wulfgar nodded slowly. 'And your powers – these things the skald told me about – are they as great as hers? Will you use them against her?'

One of the ravens fell from the trees with a shriek that startled them all, even Brochael. It perched on the branch above Kari, its eyes glinting. He held his hand up to it and let it peck at his finger. 'I'll try. That's all I can say.'

Wulfgar stared at the bird. 'Then I suppose that will have to do.'

16

Too many eyes are open by day.

Brochael woke Jessa before dawn. As she struggled up she saw Thorkil sitting and talking with Wulfgar. He laughed and waved to her.

'He doesn't seem to remember anything about last night,' Brochael said quietly. 'Best not to speak of it at all.'

'How can he not remember?'

'Who knows. But don't mention it.'

She nodded. 'Is Kari well?'

'Well enough. He'll carry the scar, that's all.'

Later, as she rolled her blanket, Thorkil came over. He grinned at her, and she saw that the restraint and silence that had grown on him lately was gone. He was easy, pleased with himself. The old Thorkil.

'Feeling better?' she said, suddenly glad to see him.

He shrugged, surprised. 'A bit tired.' He did not mention the missing arm-ring, but she saw his fingers restlessly rubbing at the white wrinkled scar that twisted about his wrist. It had not faded in the night; she wondered now if it ever would. They'll both carry scars, she thought.

All morning they moved swiftly on through the

trees, downhill, with Wulfgar scouting ahead and Brochael, like a great shadow at Kari's shoulder, keeping guard at the back. The forest was quiet, in an end-of-winter hush, brushed at its edges by a dusting of green; the tight furled buds barely splitting, the new growth of pines and firs soft and fresh among the dark needles.

When the forest ended they saw a low green valley before them, with a swift river running through it.

'This is the Skolka,' Brochael said. 'Beyond it, up in those rocks, is the Jarl's Gate, the pass down into the Mjornir district, where the Jarlshold is.'

Jessa looked up at the narrow peaks. 'I can't see any pass.'

'It's narrow,' Wulfgar said. 'Barely a thread between the rocks. A few weeks ago it would still have been blocked with snow.'

'And how do we cross the river?' Thorkil wondered.

Brochael looked at Wulfgar. 'There's a ford . . .'

'Guarded. She's not such a fool as that.'

'She's not a fool at all,' the skald muttered to Jessa, with a lopsided grin.

'You and I will have to find a place to cross,' Brochael decided. 'The rest of you can wait, and rest.'

'I'll come,' Thorkil said.

Brochael's eyes flickered doubtfully to Kari, but the boy nodded. There was nothing to worry about now, Jessa thought. They could trust him again.

'All right,' Brochael said. 'But stay close.'

When they were gone, Jessa and Kari lay in the edges of the forest, listening to Skapti's tale of his journey. The sun became almost warm; one or two early flies buzzed in the leaves. Kari fed the ravens scraps of dried meat, one perched on each side as he lay against the tree.

When the skald had finished, Jessa said, 'You might have told me – at Wormshold.'

'Not my secret. Besides' – he winked at Kari – 'we had to find out if you were safe to trust.'

'How did you know all about it?'

Skapti shrugged. 'I knew Brochael years ago. When she sent him to Thrasirshall we all heard of it. No one thought we would see him again. There was much fighting at the time . . . but later, one time when I was travelling near Trond, I decided to see him.'

'You went to Thrasirshall on your own?' Jessa was astonished.

The skald grinned. 'Oh, I was scared enough. When I saw the place I thought my heart would stop. But I knew Brochael would starve unless he had food brought in. I might add, he was glad to see me. Tired of eating rat, I suppose.'

Jessa giggled.

'I didn't see this creature' – he tapped Kari with his foot – 'until later, but a skald knows that many things that seem true are not, and all about lying. I don't think I really believed her stories, even then. We arranged a supply line for food; some of the Wulfings' men brought it, when they could get through the snow. All secret. I was there quite often after that.' He grinned. 'I remember the time this one first heard music.'

Kari nodded slowly. 'So do I . . .'

When the others came back they were wet and hungry.

'There's a place,' Brochael said, swallowing a great chunk of oatcake, 'a little way upstream. Plenty of rocks, though the current is swift and deep in places.' He spat out a piece of cheese. 'Rancid! Food is something else we need.'

'There's a house over there,' Jessa said. They looked in the direction she pointed, at the thin trail of smoke rising into the sky.

'Too dangerous,' the skald muttered.

'Unless we steal, as Odin stole the mead of Wisdom.'

'I don't steal from my own people,' Wulfgar said sharply.

Skapti laughed, rubbing his long nose. 'Then just ask, my lord. When they know it's the next Jarl at the door, they'll give.'

Wulfgar laughed at Jessa. 'Do you see the impudence I have to put up with?'

The crossing place Brochael had found was sheltered, with a few trees. The bank shelved down, but the bed of the stream was choked with rocks, the swift brown water roaring over and through them. That would be easy. But between the last rock and the further shore was at least six foot of empty, swirling water.

Brochael took off his pack, coat and shirt and tied a heavy, hempen rope around his waist. Thorkil wound the end round a rock and braced it. The big man laughed. 'It'll take more than you. If I go in I'll want you all on there.' With a glance at Kari he began to cross the rocks swiftly, with easy steps. Despite his size he was light-footed. On the last one he paused. Wulfgar and Thorkil gripped the rope. Slowly, Brochael lowered himself into the icy water. It rose high against his chest. He waded forward, and the current caught him; he staggered, fought for balance, arms wide.

Slowly he steadied, the brown water racing past him, his skin tinged with blue, as if bruised with cold. He forced his bulk through the stream, gripped the other bank and heaved himself up, the water running from him.

'Well stepped!' the skald yelled, flinging over his clothes.

Shaking with cold Brochael dressed, then he whipped the rope up from the water and tightened it, a dripping, taut line over the river. They threw the baggage over, then Kari crossed, gripping the rope tight with both hands, the birds cawing anxiously over his head. He had to drag himself, hand over hand, the current tearing at him, Brochael leaning out so far to help that he almost overbalanced. Jessa saw the raw blue scar on Kari's chest as he was pulled out. He flung his cloak on and crouched, coughing, on the bank.

Skapti crossed next, then Thorkil. As he was half-way over, the ravens croaked and rose up, circling. Kari looked up. 'They're here!'

At the end of the forest something was moving; as Jessa turned she saw a man step out, the weapon in his hand gleaming in the sun. He turned at once and shouted.

'Hurry up!' Brochael roared, leaning over and hauling Thorkil out. 'Jessa! Quick!'

With a slither of steel Wulfgar had his sword out. He turned to face the wood; already a line of men were running towards him. Jessa pulled off her coat and flung it over, scrambling from rock to rock. She tugged her boots off, threw them to Thorkil, and jumped straight into the stream.

The icy water drove the breath right out of her; she grabbed the taut rope and hung there, gasping, feeling the flow of the river against her body, filling her nose and mouth. Hand over hand, she pulled herself through the stream; her feet dragged again and again off the stones, her clothes heavy with the icy water. She heard a splash behind her; a shout. Wulfgar was on the rocks. Her hands were sore on the rope; she slipped, and grabbed tight. Then Brochael's arm gripped her. She reached up to the bank and hauled herself out, coughing and shivering. Someone flung a coat around her. She pushed the wet hair from her eyes.

Two men had outrun the others. Swords out, they were hacking at Wulfgar. Dodging, he kicked one in the ribs; the man gasped, and slipped backwards. Wulfgar leapt across the rocks; with an enormous splash he was in the water.

Brochael whirled round. 'Run. Get up to the pass!'

Already Wulfgar was halfway across, the water roaring over his clenched hands and the tight, thrumming rope. Gudrun's man slipped and slithered on the rocks, ducking stones that Skapti hurled at him. His knife flashed. With a sharp slash he brought it down on the rope, slicing through it. In an instant Wulfgar was downstream, whirled away in the roaring brown flood, battered against the rocks, clutching at the roots of trees and the brown soil.

Brochael raced after him, flung himself at full length and grabbed. Wulfgar sank and surged up, gasping. Their hands met, gripped tight, Brochael was jerked forward.

'Hold me!' he yelled, and Thorkil and Skapti threw themselves over him, clawing at his feet, and at the stems of bushes and thorns. Stones were falling on them like hail; on the far bank Gudrun's men clambered swiftly over the rocks.

'Pull!' Brochael roared. 'Pull!' Tugging on his belt and feet and shoulders, they dragged at him; hauling his own weight and Wulfgar's painfully in, inch by inch. A stone hit Thorkil on the chest; he gasped, but hung on.

Then a man screamed. Looking up, Jessa saw the ravens hurtle down, stabbing at the men's faces, fluttering and beating them with their heavy black wings, shrieking high karks of anger. The men ducked, covered their eyes. One had blood running from his forehead.

Jessa grabbed at Thorkil and heaved. Slowly, Brochael was squirming and wriggling back, and then Wulfgar grabbed the skald's hand, and with a great rush of water they dragged him out, blue with cold and shivering uncontrollably. He collapsed on to his knees, coughing and retching, but Brochael hauled him up. 'You can drown later. Come on!'

Then he turned his head.

Jessa realized, with a sudden chill, that the clamour of the birds had stopped.

Kari was standing at the bank of the stream, one raven on a rock above him, the other at his feet, silently wiping its beak in the grass. On the other side of the river, Gudrun's men were gazing at him. They stared, silent and fascinated.

'Ah,' said the skald softly. 'Look at that. Gudrun's word-hoard works against her.'

The men stood silent; one touched an amulet that swung from his coat. Then their leader whirled on them. 'Move! Get down to the ford!'

The men turned. 'You'd better hurry,' the man said grimly. 'No outlaw reaches the Jarlshold, not while I hold the passes.' He was a tall man; his eyes blue. He wore the silver snake-ring round his arm. He ran after his men. Wulfgar coughed and spat, watching him go.

'No outlaw will,' he remarked.

17

Fire is needed by the newcomer
Whose knees are frozen numb;
Meat and clean linen a man needs
Who has fared across the fells.

As they ran towards the hills they were all numb with the cold. Kari kept coughing. Brochael watched him anxiously. Their clothes clung to them; the icy winds coming down from the pass froze the sodden materials and frosted coat and shirt with tiny crystals. In the shelter of some rocks they stopped and crouched.

'We should keep on,' Thorkil said. 'They'll be coming . . .'

'It's a good long way to the ford. And we need food, and a fire,' Brochael told him.

'Then we try the homestead we saw.' Skapti stood up. 'It was this way.'

As cautiously as they could they came through the undergrowth and saw before them, as if it squatted among the rocks at the base of the mountain, a small, crooked house built of turves, its roof green and overgrown. Thorns and brambles grew up around the door; the byres looked empty and unused. Smoke drifted from the hearth-hole.

'Hardly a palace,' the skald remarked.

Wulfgar shrugged. 'I'll try and put up with it.'

The skald turned to Brochael. 'Let me go. Poets wander in strange places.'

'Not alone,' Brochael said. 'We don't know how many live there, or whether they're Gudrun's men or not. Jessa, go with him. His daughter, shall we say?'

She gave him a wry smile. 'I suppose I look poor enough.'

'I'm honoured,' Skapti laughed.

Brochael clapped him on his shoulder. 'Now look, if there's danger, get out. Don't mention us until you're sure.'

The skald nodded. He stood up, tall and thin, and Jessa followed him, the almost-empty pack slung over her shoulder. They trudged up through the rocks and the soft, wet tussocks of grass.

A bleat in the bushes startled her. She turned and saw two goats, sitting away to her left. Their slitted eyes watched her as she walked, their jaws chewing without pause.

When he reached the door, Skapti winked at her. Then he thumped twice on the soft, rotting wood. He stood as tall as the eaves.

A shuffle inside kept them silent. Then, without warning, the door opened. The man who stood there was so small he scarcely reached to Jessa's shoulder. He had a narrow face and tiny sly eyes that hardly seemed to open, hooded with heavy lids. A white stubble of beard sprouted from his chin. He looked up at them both warily.

'I'm a skald, stranger,' Skapti said briskly. 'This is my daughter Jessa. We're seeking a fire and some food.'

The dwarfish man eyed them narrowly. Then, without speaking, he shuffled aside. The skald shrugged and went in, and Jessa followed him. They were both alert for an ambush, but there was none. The room was dark, cluttered, with greasy rags and rushes on the hard mud floor. They sat down by the fire, a smoky blaze that made the room stiflingly hot, but Jessa was glad of it.

The old man handed them each a slice of hard black bread, and some cheese. The cheese was very strong, but Jessa ate it quickly. Faint steam rose from her wet clothes.

'Your girl's damp,' the old man remarked, squatting on a stool.

'The ford,' Skapti said, chewing his bread.

'Ah.' The old man stirred the fire. 'That's odd. I thought you came the other way.'

There was silence for a moment. Jessa, thinking of the others out in the cold, and Gudrun's swordsmen hurrying to the ford, wished the skald would hurry. The old man glanced at her. 'Now your girl's restless,' he said. She smiled warily.

At last Skapti said, 'I hear the Jarl Ragnar is dead.'

The old man looked up. 'News travels fast.'

'To those who are interested. You didn't tell us your name.'

Scratching his shoulder with a long hand, the old man grinned. 'You're the strangers. You speak.'

'My name is Skapti Arnsson. I was the Wulfings' poet.'

For a moment Jessa thought he had made a mistake, but she knew time was short.

123

The old man gave him a hard look. 'The Wulfings. I thought they were all dead.'

'All but one. Wulfgar. He should be Jarl, by right.'

Suddenly the old man stood. He fetched a small stone bottle, and uncorking it, poured out a hot red liquid into three cups. They drank, and it burned Jessa's throat and glowed inside her. The old man slammed his cup down and wiped his beard. 'That's what I keep for enemies of the witch. Now, let's grip like wrestlers and stop the circling. My name is Asgrim; they call me the Dwarf. How many of you are there, and who pursues you?'

Astonished, Skapti stared at him. Then he laughed. 'Well, I'm not as sly as is thought, it seems. There are four others. One is Wulfgar.'

'Outside?'

'Not far. Gudrun's men are behind us. We need to cross the pass, but first we need food and warmth.'

'Then get them in! Girl, go and get them.'

She glanced at Skapti, who shrugged. 'Do as he says.' He grinned at the old man. 'Six to one is good enough odds.'

Jessa tugged open the door and ran across the grass. Instantly she saw them coming, rising like ghosts from the bushes. 'Come on!' she called.

'How many?' Brochael asked as he came up.

'One old man.'

He nodded, and tugged her hair.

The old man glanced at Thorkil and Brochael as they ducked under the low door. Then he stabbed a finger at Wulfgar. 'You're the Wulfing, lord?'

'I am.'

'Then remember Asgrim when you're Jarl. But if they catch you, forget you ever knew me.'

Wulfgar laughed, and nodded, and pushed past him to the fire. As he moved, the old man saw Kari. Jessa had never seen anyone stand so still. After a while Kari said, 'You'll know me again.'

'Who on the gods' earth are you?' the old man whispered.

Brochael hauled Kari towards the fire. 'Get the wet clothes off – all of you! Hurry.' As he unlaced his own great shirt he grinned at the dwarf. 'He's Kari Ragnarsson. As you've guessed.

Asgrim sat down. His eyes followed Kari with fascination. 'He's her image,' he muttered. 'Every hair of his head. Every look of his eyes.'

Kari gave him a quick glance. 'That's enough,' Brochael snapped. 'Now, we'd be grateful for something to eat.'

Shaking his head, the old man got up and put more bread and cheese and cups on the table. 'Poor fare for lords,' he said, 'but it's all that's here.'

When they were dressed and warm they ate hungrily. Wulfgar swallowed a crust and said, 'If I can ever repay you, master, I will, and generously. Rings and horses will be yours for this.'

The old man grinned. 'I can't eat promises. Nor do they keep me warm.' He pointed down at the heap of wet clothes on the floor. 'I'll take these, to be going on with.'

He fingered the fine cloth of Thorkil's shirt, then picked up Brochael's tattered one. The big man roared. 'It'll go around you twice!'

'All the warmer.' The dwarf winked at them, and they laughed, until Kari said, 'Quiet.'

He lifted his eyes from the wine in his cup. 'They're outside.'

'I heard nothing,' the old man began, but Brochael waved him silent.

At the window Skapti eased back a corner of the shutter. It was getting dark outside. The trees were black shadows.

'Can't see anything.'

'They're out there,' Kari muttered. 'A lot of them.'

In the silence they heard a strange, quiet rattle and caw from the roof. 'Send the birds off,' Brochael snapped. 'They may follow.' He turned to Asgrim. 'Is there a back door?'

'They'll see you.'

'We've no choice.'

'He could hide us,' Thorkil put in.

'And have that witch torment me for it?'

Skapti laughed. 'No hero this, is he? There'll be no songs about Asgrim, I can see that.'

With a sliver of steel Brochael drew a long knife. 'Decide now. And be quick.'

'No,' Wulfgar caught his arm and forced it down. 'No. Let him choose freely. I'll not raise my hand against my host.'

For a moment Brochael glared at him. Then he nodded, and put the knife away. 'As you say. But you may have doomed us all.'

'I don't think so.' Wulfgar turned to the dwarf. His voice was slow, almost lazy. 'Now. Where's this loyalty to the Wulfings that you boast of?'

The old man scratched his beard, and laughed ruefully. 'It's over here, lord, behind this wall.' He led them through the dark room into the cow-byre next door, its floor covered with filthy straw and smelling of rats. One wall was boarded with wood;

126

he pulled a plank away to show a large space behind. 'My bolt hole. I've used it myself before now. You may not all fit.'

Brochael pushed Kari in without a word, and then Jessa. Skapti followed, folding himself up, and then Thorkil and Wulfgar. When Brochael squeezed in too there was barely room. Hurriedly Asgrim put the plank back; they heard him fling straw against it.

There was a loud thump on the outer door. Then it burst open. Voices came through, loud and threatening.

'Be ready,' Brochael whispered. 'We may have to take them by surprise.'

Jessa heard knives drawn in the darkness. Useless, she thought. If he betrays us here we're finished. Some light filtered through a knot-hole in the wood. Brochael leaned forward and blocked it, putting his eye to the hole. 'Six . . . seven,' he mouthed. 'More outside.'

'Outlaws,' they heard a voice saying. 'Traitors to the Jarl.'

'I've not seen them.' Asgrim's voice sounded near; in the doorway to the byre. 'And why should they come here?'

'They'd need food.'

'I don't have enough for myself, master, without giving to passers-by.'

'I see. And so what are these?'

Brochael jerked back from the hole.

'What is it?' Jessa asked. She saw him turn his head in the dimness.

'We left the clothes by the fire,' he breathed. 'They've found them.'

127

After nightfall I hurried back,
But the warriors were all awake.
Lights were burning, blazing torches,
So false proved the path.

Asgrim didn't hesitate. 'All right. I stole them.'

'Where from?'

'Out near the river. Behind some rocks.'

'But you didn't tell me.'

They heard the dwarf laugh. 'I'm a poor man, master. That's good cloth – well, some of it is. Your quarry must have whipped off their wet clothes and dressed in dry, then sped off and left these. They'll be halfway up the pass by now.'

There was a pause. He doesn't believe it, Jessa thought.

Then they heard Asgrim yelp in pain. 'You're a poor liar,' the warrior growled. 'They've been here, haven't they? Any idea what she'll do to you for this? I believe the silver mines beyond Ironwood always need men.'

'Believe me,' the dwarf gasped, 'I can imagine. But no outlaws have been here, I can say that for a truth.'

'Back!' Brochael muttered. 'They're coming in.'

'Search this!' The leader's voice was so near it

made Jessa jump. 'All of it. Burn the place if you have to.' The noise of smashing wood and flung furniture made Wulfgar grit his teeth. 'We can't let them do this.'

'I think,' the skald remarked drily, 'I can let them, if I force myself.'

The noise came nearer. Something began to thump the panels of their hiding place. Jessa bit her lip. No one breathed. The hand slithered along the wood, feeling. Brochael raised his axe; it glinted in the dimness.

But before he could move, there was a sudden commotion and yells from outside. A breathless voice rang in the byre.

'The birds! They're up over the pass!'

Scuffles, the slam of a door, running footsteps. Then silence.

Brochael moved first. 'Now,' he growled. He kicked down the panel with one blow and was out, pulling the others after him. A shuffle in the next room made Wulfgar turn, but it was only the old man, his head around the door. 'Hurry,' he said. 'They may be back.'

Wulfgar gripped his hand. 'I don't forget my promises.'

The small man grinned. 'You'll probably be dead. And I'll get no horses from her, either.'

Wulfgar thumped his arm and was gone. As the others passed, Asgrim spoke to Kari. 'She must fear you. You must be the one who can defeat her.'

Kari turned, bleakly. 'What about my fear of her?' he said.

Then Brochael pushed him out. 'Will you be safe, old man?'

'Safer than you.'

Brochael nodded ruefully. 'There may be songs about you, after all,' he said. Then he raced after the others.

They ran through the trees until the ground began to slope upwards. Behind a pile of boulders Brochael stopped them. He crouched, one great arm round Thorkil's shoulder. 'Listen. We go silent and we go swift. They're ahead of us, and will have men watching every path. They'll also be waiting at the pass, but there's no other way over, and we must take it. Be wary; keep your eyes open.'

They nodded.

'No one is to carry anything. Throw those empty packs in here.' He pulled some bushes apart and they tossed in the bags, the springy growth swishing back as he let it go. 'Now. Take care.'

They climbed slowly, following the course of a narrow rocky stream that tumbled down the slope into the river. It cut deep into the peaty soil; thick tangles of gorse and bramble sprawled across it. They went carefully in the gathering darkness, often on hands and knees, keeping their heads low, below the level of the bank, splashing through the brown tumbling water chock-full of rocks. When the stream became smaller and dwindled to a trickle things were more difficult. This high up, the ground was open; only boulders and the shadows of stunted trees offered cover. They crawled in the dark over the boggy ground, flattening at any sound, until Jessa's clothes were wet and her nostrils full of the smells of the mosses and the tiny creeping plants, the tussocky grass and the sundew that clung to her hair.

As the mountainside rose and became rockier,

they began to clamber among loose boulders that dislodged and tumbled underfoot, and scree that slid treacherously. Once, the skald nearly fell, and only Thorkil's quick grip kept him up. The wind became colder, the air damp with thin rain. There were few signs of Gudrun's men. Wulfgar thought they had crossed the mountains already, but Brochael just grunted. Jessa knew he was worried about the pass; that the danger would be up there, in the narrowest place.

He was right.

As midnight crept on and the sky turned black, they saw up ahead of them in the rainy air the red sparks of fires, the flickering shadows of watchers.

Finally, crouching behind a tower of rock, they saw the pass. It was a very narrow place, where the path dwindled to a thread between two pinnacles of the mountain, sheer and jagged. In the very middle of the path a fire had been lit; men sat around it, talking, the edges of their faces red in the flamelight. Beyond, in the darkness, the path must run on, over the lip of the hill, down and down, into the flat marshy country of the Jarlshold.

Brochael took a long look, then turned his back and leaned against the rock, stretching out his legs in front of him. 'We'll need the High One himself to get us through this.'

Thorkil turned to Kari. 'Why don't you do what you did before – make us invisible.'

Kari shook his head. 'That's not what I did. I made one man think he had not seen you. There are far too many of them for that. I can't touch all their minds.'

Thorkil shrugged. 'So what can you do?' There

131

was a touch of scorn in his voice. Jessa remembered the unwinding arm-ring and frowned at him. But then he didn't remember.

'I don't know,' Kari said. 'Not yet.'

After a silence Wulfgar rubbed his wet hair. 'We can't get by with stealth, so we must attack.'

'No.' Brochael shook his head. 'We'd be cut to pieces.'

'Well, do you have any other ideas?'

'None.'

There was another silence. Finally Jessa said, 'I've got an idea.' They all looked at her. She was fiddling with the laces on her boots. 'It's the fire.'

'What about it?' Wulfgar asked patiently.

'It's the only light they've got. And it's what blocks the way. If the fire went out suddenly, it would be dark, very dark, in that crack in the rocks. Their eyes wouldn't be used to it. We could take them by surprise, if we were near enough.'

Brochael was nodding. 'Yes, she's right.'

'But listen, little shamanka,' the skald said, pulling gently on her hair, 'how do we put it out? Throw rocks at it?'

She shrugged. 'Kari must put it out.'

Kari looked at her. 'I've told you, I can't . . .'

'I don't mean make them believe. I mean put it *out*. You, yourself.' She shuffled round to look at him, her voice urgent. 'She could do it, and if she could, you can. You must. You must know your own powers.'

Kari stared into the darkness. He let Brochael put a hand on his shoulder. 'What do you think?' the big man asked gently.

'I don't know. I'll try, but . . .'

132

'You can,' Jessa said quietly. 'And you know it.'

He smiled. 'If you say so.'

'If it was possible,' Brochael said slowly, 'we could be through in seconds. Wulfgar and I will hold the pass until you're down.' He grinned at the dark man sprawled elegantly in the mud. 'What do you say, my lord? We'd have some good fighting.'

Wulfgar nodded, but the skald said softly, 'I thought the point of this was a new Jarl. Not much use to us if he's dead.'

Wulfgar ignored him. 'So it depends on you, rune-master,' he said to Kari.

Kari turned and gazed over the rocks at the blaze of fire. 'Let's move up closer, then.'

Shadows in the darkness, they drifted from rock to rock, silent as ghosts. Now they were so near they could hear the soft speech of the watchers, and the crackle and spit of flames. A sentinel moved past them; they waited, flat against rock. Kari, a darker shape in the darkness, edged out so that he could see the flames. Jessa saw the light of them glimmer on his face.

They waited, unmoving. For a while nothing changed; they had time to know they were crouched in a dark, damp place high up on a mountain, pinned down by the wind.

And then Jessa began to feel it, a slow accumulation of darkness, a gathering up of night from all its cracks and holes and crannies. Kari was conjuring with black air; as he lay flat against the rock, unmoving, she could sense his mind searching, gathering, piling night on night.

The fire glimmered. A man muttered something and threw on kindling; sparks flew and went out.

Above the flames the air seemed a web of blackness, descending, drifting down. The red light grew less. The flames sank. Kari clenched his fists, his face intent. 'Go on,' Jessa breathed, half to herself. 'Go on.' Slowly the fire was dwindling, shrinking to small cold blue flames. Someone shouted angrily; the charred sticks were stirred into a cloud of ash. Kari gripped Brochael's sleeve.

'Now,' he said. And the fire went out.

It was gone so suddenly that Jessa was barely ready. In the blackness someone pushed her. She sprang up and ran up the steep path, slipping between shadows in a confusion of shouts and the clash of swords. Someone grabbed her; she thumped at his chest and shoved him away, and then she was over the pass and racing downhill over loose stones that clattered and spilled under her feet; down and down into the darkness of the land below. Breathless with speed, she slid and rolled, and grabbed at the scree to steady herself, hearing the stones rattle down and fall, a long way. She crouched on hands and knees. Someone was kneeling at her side. 'All right?'

She recognized Thorkil's voice. 'Yes.' She scrambled up. 'Where are they?'

The top of the mountain was black against the dim sky. Figures moved up there; there were shouts, the ominous clang of metal.

'Brochael's holding them.' Thorkil sounded breathless, choked with excitement. 'He and Wulfgar, like they said!'

'They'll be killed! Where's Kari?'

'I don't know.'

She looked up. 'We must do something!'

134

But as they watched it, the sky split open. An arch of blue light flamed suddenly over the hilltop, and under it they saw Brochael clearly, wielding his axe, scattering men, and Wulfgar, his sword flashing blue and purple. Then out of the arch shot strange shafts of eerie fire, glimmering down like a net of light. Gudrun's men leapt back, one yelling, as the blue flames scorched him, until the rippling curtain of light had closed the pass. Wulfgar and Brochael were already hurtling down the path to where Jessa and Thorkil waited.

'Where's Kari?' Brochael gasped.

'Here.' He was standing further down the slope, the skald at his side.

In the eerie blue light Brochael stared at him. 'Did you do that?' he said, his voice gruff. 'How could you have done that?'

Kari was silent. Then he said, 'I didn't want you to be hurt.'

Brochael shoved his axe into his belt. For a moment Jessa thought she saw something new in his face; some fear. But when he looked up at Kari it was gone. 'Let's get on,' he said.

19

Learned I grew then, lore-wise,
Waxed and throve well.
Word from word gave words to me,
Deed from deed gave deeds to me.

They moved down the hillside, a line of shadows in the darkness. No one pursued them. For hours, looking back, they could see the strange gate of blue light on the hilltop, dwindling behind them, until they came down to the trees and it was lost among the branches. Jessa was at the back, near Brochael. 'What happened up there?' she asked quietly.

He shrugged. 'It came down between us – between her men and us. Fire, sparkling, spitting, crackling. It was like lightning that stayed. I tell you, Jessa, it scares me. I never thought he could do that.'

Silent, she nodded. But it didn't scare her. It filled her with secret, fierce delight. Oh, Gudrun, she thought, wait until you see what we're bringing you!

That night they stopped and slept near the banks of a stream, lulled by the wind in the trees and the trickle of meltwater. In the morning they moved on, always down, into the endless forests. As the day went on the sky darkened. A coldness in the air seemed to thicken and drift together; it made a low mist that wrapped itself around the boles of trees.

As the travellers walked it swirled cold and wet about their legs, soaking coats and cloaks and Jessa's skirts.

'Witch-mist,' the skald remarked over his shoulder. 'This is her welcome.'

Brochael called them to stop and looked, as he always did, at Kari. 'Is he right?' he asked.

Kari was leaning against a tree. He seemed to grow more silent the further they went. As he nodded, drops of dew ran from his hair. 'She's watching us. Her face is white among the candles. She'll deal with us herself now.'

As he spoke the mist drifted between them, muffling sound, ice-cold on the skin. 'Keep together,' Brochael said quickly. 'Within touch, or we're lost.'

Jessa felt his strong fingers fasten on her belt. She gripped Thorkil's wrist. 'Where's Wulfgar?'

'Right here.' A shadow moved at the skald's side; his voice strangely echoless in the mirk.

'What now?' Thorkil said.

'We go on. Hand in hand, if necessary.'

'We can't move in this, Brochael,' Wulfgar said quietly. 'We've no way of telling our direction; we could go miles out of our way.'

'We can't afford to wait either,' Jessa put in. 'Not if you want to be the next Jarl.'

She heard Skapti chuckle. 'Sharply put,' he whispered in her ear.

She turned to Kari. 'What about the birds? They'll fly above this – can't we follow them?'

She saw him nod. He gave a call and the two black shapes dropped heavily through the trees, one with its huge talons digging into the leather of his gloves. The other hopped to a fallen log and screeched.

'What are these creatures?' Wulfgar asked. 'Birds or spirits?'

Kari glanced at him. 'They said Odin has two ravens. One is Thought, and one is Memory. They see all that passes in the world.' He threw one up into the mist and the other followed.

When they moved on they kept together, following the high, distant kark of the two ravens. Fog clung to their faces and drifted into their mouths when they spoke; it slithered about them, cold and white. None of them could see where they were going, or noticed that the forest was beginning to thin out, until the ground underfoot became marshy, with tussocks of grass that tripped them up. Their feet sank into soft mud.

The croaks of the ravens were growing fainter, far to the left. Then they faded away. Kari called, twice, but nothing answered.

Finally they stopped. Silence and cold closed in around them, like a silver ring. Jessa remembered Mord's tale of the white mist that had swallowed the Jarl's men, long ago; of how they marched into it and not one had come out. Was that how it would be now, for them? A crystal of snow floated down on to her glove; a strange star with seven points. It melted slowly into the soft leather.

'We're out of the woods.' Brochael pulled his hand from his glove and rubbed his beard and hair. 'No more than a few miles from the Jarlshold. There will be men waiting.'

'How do you know?' Thorkil asked curiously.

'Salt, lad. I can smell the water of the fjord. I've been a long time away from it.'

He grinned at Jessa but she only said, 'It's snow.'

138

They stared at her.

'She's sending snow.' Jessa looked up. 'And the birds are lost in it.'

Silent, they watched it come spinning down around them; soft wet flakes falling on hair and in the folds of clothes. It glittered, like silver.

'Don't taste it,' Kari said slowly. 'Don't let it touch your lips.'

Wulfgar untied the scarf from his neck and wrapped it around his face. They all did the same, muffling nose and mouth.

'Now keep on,' Brochael snapped. 'This witch-brew won't keep us back.' He pushed Thorkil forward and they hurried behind him, splashing into freezing pools and marsh-mire. Already the snow was horizontal; it was a white storm in their eyes and faces.

Jessa saw Kari slip, and waited. 'All right?'

He nodded, his eyes shards of grey. 'This is for me.'

'This?'

'The snow. All of it.' For a moment he stood still. 'And the worst will be seeing her. All those silent days . . .'

'That's all over.'

He shook his head. 'That silence lives with you. You can never fill it.'

She nodded, not knowing what to say. They moved on slowly, behind the others.

'What do you want,' he said, 'if we get through all this?'

'Wulfgar to be Jarl. And my farm back. Horolfstead. It's near the sea. What do you want?'

Snow stuck to his hair and eyelids. 'I want not to be like her.'

'But you're not!'

'I am. I'm afraid she will make me part of herself.' He turned to her. 'Does that sound strange? But she can do that. Suck you in, burrow into your heart – '

A yell interrupted him. As Jessa whirled round she saw men leap out of the snow. Two of them clung to Brochael, who roared and flung them off, but before he could tug out his axe they had grabbed him and pulled him down.

'Keep still,' Kari muttered.

Wulfgar and the skald were already surrounded; Thorkil had his sword knocked scornfully into the marsh – he swore and struggled but a blow in the chest silenced him.

'Only six,' Kari muttered.

'Can they see us?'

'Not us.'

They were Gudrun's men; they wore the snake-rings on their wrists. One of them dragged Thorkil up. 'The Jarl's son. Where is he?' Breathless, Thorkil shook his head. The man flung him on to Brochael. 'Spread out. She said we might not see him.'

They moved quickly, making a ring of swords. Kari and Jessa were inside it.

'Cut the air. Use your swords. He's here.'

'You're wasting your time,' Brochael snarled, but they took no notice and began to close in, moving together through the blizzard. Blades sliced the swirling snow.

Jessa took a step back. 'The one on the left,' she breathed.

But the man heard; his eyes widened with terror.

140

'Here!' he yelled, flinging one arm out. He touched Jessa's hair and grabbed at it. She screamed and kicked him, and as he staggered back Skapti stuck out his long leg and tripped him so that he crashed to the ground. At once Jessa and Kari had leapt through the gap and raced into the flying web of snow.

'Run!' Brochael yelled.

They ran blindly, stumbling through the wet fen, the cries and shouts behind them dying into wind and silence; ran until their lungs ached and they collapsed behind a heap of stones, coughing and dragging in breath.

'We can't go back for them,' Kari gasped. 'There's no time.' She saw him turn, his hands clenched.

'Can you hear it?' he asked savagely.

'The wind?'

'It's not the wind, it's her, taunting me. She's waiting for me to come. She wants it!'

Jessa shoved the knife back in her belt. 'I know. And we've all helped her.'

'You?'

'Even me,' Jessa said bitterly. 'I was so proud – I thought I'd outwitted her. I wouldn't let her use me – I threw the arm-ring away. But it didn't matter. She made us bring you – she's let us come, through the snow and the mist, through the fingers of her men. She wants you for something.'

Kari gave her a strange look. 'You think so?'

'So does Brochael.'

He lifted his head. 'Then let's not disappoint her.'

It was her snow. They walked through a white moving tunnel of it, and it stung on the skin like venom. Dimly, on each side, shapes flickered,

141

shifted and came to nothing – wolves, worms, troll-shadows that danced in the corners of their eyes – but they walked on swiftly to the place where the snow ended, and stepped through the edge of it, into darkness.

Before them the sky was purple, dotted with faint stars. They looked over a wide stretch of marshy ground, misty with gases and smokes that rose from the earth, the smell of them drifting on the wind. Not far off the plop of some creature into a pool sounded loud and strange.

Across the marsh stood the Jarlshold: a cluster of black roofs, with the carven ends of the Hall gables clear against the sky. There were no lights down there, no sounds. Not even the barking of a dog.

Without speaking, they began to move forward, helping each other over the treacherous mire. The water was brackish and icy, with a sharp smell of weed and decay. Strange tiny lights, purple and green and blue, moved among the reeds and mists, always at a distance.

Jessa's skirt slopped against her boots; her hair was muddy and clung to her back. The fumes of the marsh made them cough, and the sound echoed through the stillness.

Gradually the ground rose, became drier. They climbed a long slope of thorn and black, spiny bushes, and pushed through them on to a track paved with flat stones.

As they followed it between the first houses, their footsteps sounded loud in the stillness. There was no watchman, no challenge. Jessa wondered how late it was, whether everyone was asleep, but the silence was not normal. And no smoke. That meant no fires in the houses.

They passed Mord's house, but the door was closed and she dared not try it. The shadows between the buildings were black; as they came silently under the walls of the great Hall, Jessa saw that the windows were shuttered, and no light leaked from them. The two ravens, like gargoyles, were perched on the roof. One gave a short kark.

'Where is everyone?' she asked. 'What's she done with them?'

'Nothing. They're here.'

'How do you know?'

Kari did not seem to hear. He took her hand, and they moved silently along the black wall.

At the door the watchman's stool was empty, and there was no dog. Jessa put her hand to the door and lifted the latch. It moved easily, with a tiny creak that made her wince. Both together, they pushed it ajar, and slipped inside.

20

Offered, myself to myself.

Gudrun was waiting for them.

She was standing with her back to the fire; the smoke of it hung about her in the dark spaces of the Hall.

No one spoke. Kari leaned with his back against the door, hands behind him; then, slowly, he walked out into the firelight. Jessa stayed where she was.

He stopped a few yards from Gudrun and they stared at each other in silence. To Jessa the likeness they shared was astonishing: the same thin paleness, the same sense of hidden power – even the same straight, shining hair, though Kari's was ragged and muddy, and Gudrun's arranged in long elaborate braids.

Then the woman moved, with a rustle of silks.

'Where are your friends?'

'Your men have them.' Kari's voice was low, but his hands were clenched and trembling. 'You should have known that.'

She shrugged lightly. 'Perhaps I did.'

'No,' he said slowly. 'You didn't.'

A flicker of expression crossed her face, as if she was surprised, but it was gone before Jessa could be sure.

144

Gudrun moved nearer to Kari. She was taller. She ran a narrow finger down his patched coat. Jessa saw, tied around her wrist, a wisp of dried snake-skin.

'Not the clothes for the Jarl's son.'

'You took that away from me.'

'I could give it back.' She smiled, with real amusement, and touched his hair. Jessa saw how he stiffened.

'It's too late.' He pulled away and went to the fire and tossed on a handful of kindling. Then he stood close up to the flames. The new wood crackled and spat; the sound echoed in the roof.

'You're afraid of me.' He said it steadily, but with an effort, looking into the leaping web of flame. 'Because I'm the same as you – just the same. You invented all those lies so that no one would know it, but they only have to look. Any powers you have I have too.'

She smiled, smoothing her dress. 'But I know how to use them. You don't.'

'I've been learning.'

'Tricks played on fools. Not the real spells, not the twisting of minds, the webs of fear and delight.'

She had come after him, and reached out again, fingering the ends of his hair as if she could not leave him alone. 'As for fear, I'm afraid of nothing.'

'Except your reflection,' Jessa said.

Gudrun turned quickly, as if she had forgotten her. 'Silence!'

'It's true.' Kari looked up. 'And you know it's not the one in the mirror. I'm your reflection.'

Gudrun was still a moment. Then she said, 'Indeed you are. You and I are the same.'

'No.' He shook his head, but she went up to him; clutched his hands.

'Look at us. Together we could make the North such a kingdom of sorcery as has never been dreamed. I have let you live for this, watched you, to see what you would become.' Her cold eyes glittered. 'And you've become me.'

'No!' Kari stepped back. 'You're wrong. I would never join with you.'

Gudrun straightened; her fingers stabbed the air; she snapped out a rune. Kari caught his breath. To Jessa's horror, he staggered with a gasp of pain.

'Stop it! Leave him alone,' she cried.

But already he was lifting his head, straightening, white and unsteady. When he spoke his voice was bitter. 'You won't do that again. Now, feel its reflection.'

He did not move, or say anything, but the witch slowly bent before him like a candle too close to heat. Her eyes widened; she staggered to the table and clutched it, one hand gripping the edge, her knuckles white.

'This is pain,' he said quietly, coming up behind her. 'This is how it feels. And these are nightmares – see them? This is silence. This is fear.'

Gudrun shuddered, shaking her head. She beat off something invisible with her hand; quick, nervous snatches. Kari stood and watched. Then he touched her hair. Jessa felt her heart thump with fear.

'Are these the webs you mean?' he said softly. 'You see I can weave them too.'

Gudrun buckled into a chair. Her long hands lay on the table – Jessa could see them trembling. The hall was dark and silent.

146

Then Kari turned away, and Gudrun's hands were still. He went back to the fire. After a while he said, in a sharp voice, 'It's over – your time of power. There are two of us now – a balance. I think you should go back to the place you came from; leave the Jarlshold to choose its own leader.'

'You?' she said scornfully, raising her head.

'Not me. They won't want me.' He rubbed his hair wearily. 'I'm too much like you.'

'Kari!' Jessa hissed.

He turned, and saw that the witch was standing, tall and pale. Her white gown fell in straight folds; it glinted like frost.

'It's not finished,' she said. 'Has he told you about the Serpent, this Brochael you're so fond of? The Serpent hugs the world; it devours itself. It will never be destroyed until the end of the world, when the great wolf of darkness snaps its binding, and the ship of monsters sails into the harbour. Far from here, far to the north, is a hall, all woven of white snakes; its doors face out to the eternal ice.'

She held out her hands; drew them slowly apart. Jessa saw light gleam between them. The hall seemed to shudder; the shutters creaked as if something was pressing against them.

'That is the place I come from,' Gudrun said. 'The Serpent is what I serve. And now it strikes.'

She was close to him; her hands moved in a flash of light. Jessa screamed, and grabbed Kari, hauling him aside as the knife slashed down. Gudrun turned and struck again; the blade whistled past Jessa's face, slicing through strands of her hair. Kari grabbed it. With an effort he wrenched it out of her hand and flung it on to the fire.

147

At once the flames roared up, higher than his head. Long coils of smoke poured out, twisting around his neck and arms. It swept around Jessa's waist, squeezing her tight, even though her hands went through it as she beat at it. She yelled and squirmed, but the serpent of smoke held her, hugging the breath out of her. Its tongue flickered at Kari, pinning him against the wall, blackening the stones and scorching the tapestry behind him into smoking holes. As he dodged, the cloth caught alight; a line of flame ran up the edge, crackling through the dusty threads.

Kari scrambled through the smoke to Jessa. As he caught hold of her the weight on her chest seemed to burst; she breathed in, sick and dizzy.

'Where is she?' he yelled, but Jessa shook her head, and jerked back as the tapestry fell, a roaring sheet of flame, from the wall.

'This way,' she screamed.

They ran to the door and tugged. It didn't move. Jessa slammed her palms against it and whirled round. 'The windows, then!'

But the windows were shuttered, the Hall a closed cage of burning cloth. Smoke stung their eyes; they were coughing and retching. High overhead the roof-tree crackled, spilling sparks like blossom.

Outside, a voice was yelling. Something thumped on the door.

Jessa slammed and kicked at it. 'How can we get out?'

'We can't.'

He dragged her down and they gasped the cold airs near the floor. Then she looked at him. To her astonishment she saw he was half smiling. She forced herself to be calm. 'What are you going to do?'

'This.'

He knelt in the smoke, his hands gripped into fists.

And the smoke turned white. It gathered itself together into hard grains and fell, silently. It fell from the darkness up there in the rafters; fell as a gentle, relentless snow, on to the flames, on to Jessa's hair and upturned face. The air grew cold; the water on her cheeks froze. Soot hardened to a black glaze, and the flames sank. Tapestries stiffened into rigid folds and hard, crumpled masses on the flagstones.

Slowly, easily, the snow fell, whitening floor and tables; hanging like frail lace on their clothes, and on Gudrun's, as she sat in the centre of the Hall, watching them.

She sat calmly in a great chair, her face expressionless. On a stool at her feet huddled the wizened old man Grettir, looking more ancient than ever. His long eyes watched them both carefully. Jessa stared back. Had they been there all the time, in all that flame and smoke?

Suddenly, someone outside yelled. The door shuddered, as if something heavy had struck it.

The witch stood up, and came forward. The old man followed her like a dog. She seemed slightly smaller, almost as if something had gone from her. Close up, Jessa saw the faint lines on her face, as she knelt, thoughtfully, by Kari.

'It seems you're right,' she said. 'There are two of us now.' She smiled at him. 'So I will do you the greatest harm I can. I'll give you what you want.'

'What do you mean?' he muttered.

149

'I leave it all to you,' she said. 'With this curse. They will never love you, never trust you. Power like ours is a terror to them. You'll see that. Your new Jarl will want to be rid of you as soon as he can.' She touched his shoulder lightly. 'And you'll use them, as I did. It's what we always do.'

Then she was on her feet, walking to the black folds of tapestry. She tugged them back, and there was the small arch Jessa remembered. The door shuddered again. Gudrun ignored it, and turned and tossed something down that rolled and lay on the stone flags. 'Keep this,' she said. 'One day I may come back for it.'

As she turned he said, 'You're wrong about me. I'm not like you.'

'We'll see,' she said. Jessa thought she was smiling. Then she was gone, the old man close behind, into the stone passages behind the curtain.

After a moment Jessa turned and ran to the door. She pulled the latch and it lifted easily; she tugged the heavy door wide. The men outside stared at her, but someone gave a great shout and grabbed her arms. She saw it was Brochael, with a crowd of others at his back.

'Where's Kari?'

'Inside.'

They surged past her. She saw Gudrun's men standing uncertain outside, but she left them and followed Thorkil.

'Where's Gudrun?' he asked.

She shook her head, suddenly tired.

Wulfgar had picked the object off the floor; he gave it to Kari, who fingered the knotted snakeskin.

150

'Search the Hold,' Brochael said, but Kari shook his head.

'You won't find her. She's gone.'

'But where?'

'Back. Wherever she came from.'

'For good?' Brochael asked gruffly.

Kari shrugged. 'That's more than I can say.' Suddenly he turned to Wulfgar. 'Well. Here we are in your Hall. It seems the Wulfings have come home at last.'

The skald went over and kicked the frozen mass of the fire.

'And not a moment too soon,' he remarked.

21

Silence becomes the son of a prince.

By morning the whole of the Jarlshold had been searched, but there was no sign of Gudrun or Grettir. How she had vanished from among them no one knew, but it was said later that a man who farmed up on the fells to the east had seen a woman, dressed all in white, walking swiftly and tirelessly over the snow, with a dark figure like a shadow behind her. Terrified, he had hurried indoors, to the firelight.

First thing in the morning the men of the Jarlshold and all the surrounding settlements had gathered in the great Hall, staring at the travellers curiously. Many of them could not tear their eyes from Kari, as he sat quietly next to Jessa at the long table. He left all the talking to Brochael and Wulfgar. Jessa knew that the presence of so many people was making him uneasy; she caught his eye and smiled and he did the same. Wulfgar was voted Jarl with a great roar of approval, no one disagreeing, but afterwards, in the crush and excitement, Kari was missing. She searched for him, pushing her way to Thorkil.

'Have you see Kari?'

He shook his head. 'Elsewhere, I suppose. Not used to all these people.'

But when she asked Brochael he paused for a moment and shrugged, a little unhappily. 'I have an idea where he might be. Come on.'

As she followed him out of the Hall, she heard silence fall behind her, and into it came the skald's voice, clear and sharp, chanting an old song in praise of the Wulfings, a chain of words, lilting and proud. Looking back, she saw Wulfgar sitting in the Jarl's chair, relaxing in it lazily, his fingers moving over the worn arms as Ragnar's had done. Behind him, Thorkil leaned.

She followed Brochael. They went down into a part of the Jarlshold she had never seen: a long dark corridor at the foot of a flight of damp steps. On each side were small rooms, their windows barred, and the stench from them stale and fetid.

'Her prisons,' Brochael growled. 'Full, till this morning.'

His voice echoed in the stone tunnel.

She followed him to the very end, deep in the rock under the Hold. The door of the last room was ajar, and he pushed it open. They saw a very small cell, long neglected. The walls were dark with grime and soot. Old straw rustled under their feet; one tiny window let in the light.

Kari stood at the far end of the room, looking at something on the wall. Jessa saw it was some faint scrawl of circles and spirals, almost worn away with age. His hair shone pale and clean, and he wore the new clothes that Wulfgar had given them all from the Jarl's store. He turned round when he heard them.

153

'Why come here?' Brochael asked gruffly.

'Just to look. To see if I remembered it right.' After a moment he took the snakeskin bracelet from his pocket and fingered it, dropping it silently into the cold ashes in the fireplace. Then he came out and closed the door.

Brochael put an arm round him. 'Come on. The lord Jarl will be having his first feast tonight. Everyone will want to stare at you as he loads you with gold and gives us all rings and horses. Asgrim will be here within days, when he hears.'

'I don't want his gold,' Kari said. 'But I would like Thrasirshall – whatever is left of it.'

Brochael nodded. 'You'll get it! Who else would want it?' He grinned at Jessa. 'And the new lady of Horolfstead will be wearing her best, I expect?'

'All borrowed,' Jessa laughed.

Kari laughed too. Then he turned and raised his hands, and made a small movement.

As they watched it, the door faded, out of sight.